TOFU COWBOY

LOLA WEST

For my Papasan

who is so loved and always in my corner

xo, your only little girl

1

LUKE

"Damn it." I slapped my hand against the steering wheel. Why did red lights always last an eternity when you're late? I could see the entrance to Fletcher Community College from where I was stopped. Usually, I got to campus early. It was a long haul to Fletcher from my hometown of Conway, Montana—about forty-five minutes. I tried to leave with time to spare, but today I got stuck with my brothers, Bill, Wyatt, and Cody, managing a few cows that got loose on the southwest corner of my family's ranch. It should have been no big deal. Just herd 'em back in. But one stubborn cow got itself stuck in the mud and it was like watching a scene outta *The Three Stooges*. First, Wyatt went bottom-up, his feet right out from under him and we all laughed. Then Cody skidded into a full belly flop. And before you knew it, I was up to my neck in sludge too. Bill sat atop his horse, snickering like a prince surrounded by jokers. We needed rope and a series of heave-hos to get the job done. It was a fiasco. And it meant that before I could leave for class, I had to run home and shower.

I wouldn't have had to be late if I had the balls to tell my family I was taking a drawing class. But the thing was, I wanted to explore my art without having it be the butt of my brothers' jokes. I secretly wanted my art to be more than a hobby. I had always loved to draw. They knew I drew, but we were ranchers, and on the ranch, my creativity made me soft. They wouldn't understand that art was my passion and I didn't want to have to explain that a real man could love to draw. So, I decided to take this class in Fletcher, which was far enough away from Conway that no one knew me, and if drawing panned out, then I would broach the subject with my family.

As soon as the light changed, I raced into the parking lot. I grabbed my supply bag, slammed my truck door, and hurried to the art studio. I crashed through the door, my boots three steps ahead of my brain. Since class had already started, the calamity of my entrance caused everyone to turn and look at me.

Feeling my cheeks heat, I said, "Sorry. So sorry," making my way through the circle of easels to the one that was mine.

Once I got into position, I rifled through my bag, looking for my pencils and charcoal. I couldn't find anything. I must have left my pencil case in the truck or at my apartment. Not sure, but they definitely weren't in my bag. It was not the first day of class, but it sure felt like it. Suddenly, I realized I was surrounded by the silence of everyone still waiting on me, and I looked up. My professor stared directly at me and asked, "Is it alright with you if we begin?"

"Please, let's get this party started," I said with a grin. Nobody corners a Morgan brother. It's not in our makeup to yield.

The sweetest sound I'd ever heard floated toward me from the podium where the bowls of fruit and vases of flowers had sat for the last month or so. It was a woman's laugh. I had forgotten we switched from still life to a live model halfway through the semester. So, not only was I late, but I put out this woman who was baring herself to us in service of art. I cringed at my cloddish behavior, took a deep breath, and turned to take in the woman that produced the sound.

All the air left my body. This woman was literally breathtaking. She was partially naked. Our professor explained that for the first few weeks she would be draped in a sheet, so short of a laurel wreath on her head, she appeared as the echo of a Greek goddess. She was curvy and buxom in a way that had my blood racing south. Everything about her was lush—full pink lips, huge ice-blue eyes, thick dark lashes, and long waves of deep-blue curls that fell across her shoulders and the tops of her barely covered breasts. In our part of the world, you don't see many women with nontraditional hair colors, so I wasn't partial per se, but something about her blue locks felt inspired, like she should have been born that way. Her skin looked like satin and my fingers ached to touch it. An urge like I'd never felt before overtook my being. I felt driven to plow through the easels, knocking them to the floor, mount the podium, take this woman, and make her mine. If she was a cupcake, I would have licked my finger and touched her to stake my claim.

Anthony, the kid that worked at the easel next to mine, leaned over and tapped my shoulder.

"Are you okay, dude?" he whispered. "Is this the first time you've ever seen a woman?" He laughed under his breath.

Then he waved his hand at me and I realized he was offering me a pencil.

I took it, and looking back at my goddess, I mumbled, "I've never seen one like that."

2

MADDIE

I sat as still as I possibly could, but I so wanted to look at the cowboy. I liked him from the minute he barreled into the room. He was a full-blown comedy of errors. Late, noisy, no pencil, a real mess, and when the professor gave him flak for being late, he swung charm at the guy, wielding his humor like a sword. For the record, a ballsy ego in the face of authority was my kind of pie.

He was a looker too. Tall, broad, resplendently manly, straight-up yum. He had that strange but tasty combo of a full dark beard and long blond hair. How did that happen and why was no one asking that question? If we saw someone with different-colored eyes, we'd all be saying wow. But genetically two-toned hair and everyone was just like, whatever. No matter, very sexy—especially to someone like me who cut and colored hair for a living.

In this art class, he stood out like a rare bird, a grown-ass adult in a sea of children with crayons and backpacks. Literally, every student except him couldn't have been more than nineteen, and they all looked like they were wearing their pajamas. But honestly, come on, how often did you see a full-blown cowboy sketching at an easel? And he was the real deal—boots, jeans, big ol' belt buckle. For the love of doughnuts, he was still wearing his hat. I could feel him looking at me. He was off to my left, exactly parallel to me, so I could see him in my peripheral vision, but not really.

Admittedly, there were a lot of eyes on me. I expected to be looked at. I chose this gig. I have been working on learning to love my body. I was a recovered anorexic/bulimic. I was not ashamed of it. I had a shit childhood and managed it in a self-destructive way. I got myself help. I've been in recovery for almost a decade. We all have our ugly, right? My only regret was that my ugly left me barren. But barren is better than dead. Recovering from an eating disorder wasn't about feeling pretty. It was about letting go of the need to control everything. So I did that, but now I wanted to feel beautiful in my skin. Hence, this whole model for an art class thing. I thought baring my skin to a room full of strangers would be a good step in owning my beauty and releasing the pressure to respond to outside judgment.

But all the eyes put together didn't hold a candle to the impact of having his gaze aimed in my direction. Something about the way he stared at me felt like he saw me in a way that others didn't. Again, I couldn't really see the dude, but his eyes acted like fingers on my skin as if he were caressing every inch of me with his glances. And I reacted as if touched, literally trembling under his examination. I am not a wallflower or a saint. I have been loved and sexed up in my life, but I have never felt a man's eyes on me like they knew the secrets of my lady bits... like never. Also, I wasn't even fully naked yet. How was I going to handle that situation?

After an hour or so, and mere minutes before I lost my cool and full-on orgasmed from the way the cowboy was looking at me, the art professor told everyone that it was time to gather their things. (By the way, the professor's first name was Rufus, which was not only a dog's name, but also a name that felt a little like it might belong to a creeper.) I still didn't move. I didn't know if I was supposed to. Also, I was a little confused by what was going to happen to the sheet that I was draped in when I stood up. I wasn't naked underneath. I was wearing underwear and a strapless bra, but still, I remained unsure of the protocol. In the movies, artist's models always have silky kimono robes. Clearly, I failed to adequately prepare for my role. I wondered where I could get one before my next appearance as muse extraordinaire. Not in Conway.

Slowly, one by one, the Crayola crowd packed up their things and filtered out of the room. The cowboy was the only one left. He approached Rufus. I was so eavesdropping.

With a gentle, humble tone, he said, "Listen, man, I'm sorry if I gave you attitude. I hate being late, and it's not my MO. It won't happen again."

Rufus was a consummate dick. "Lateness is not tolerated in this space, Mr. Morgan. In the future, you will kindly refrain from entering if tardy."

Arguments with pompous blowhards like Rufus were a waste, but if the cowboy was hotheaded, Rufus' self-important air might set him off. Inexplicably, I wanted to save him from the kerfuffle of upsetting his professor. I pushed my chair back and stood, bringing their attention to me. With the sheet pressed to my chest, I asked, "Do I just like get dressed now? Or do I wait for you two to leave?"

Rufus smiled his subtly douchey smile. "Our apologies, Madeline. We will give you some privacy. We'll see you next week."

It's Madison, not Madeline, but whatever, Professor McStuffy.

He snapped his artsy leather briefcase closed and headed for the door.

The cowboy, Mr. Morgan, was slower to move, like it hurt him to take his eyes off me, but he also walked to the door, leaving me alone in the room.

I quickly got dressed and headed out. No need to dawdle. The halls of the building were as empty as a toy store on the day after Christmas, and every one of my footsteps echoed on the linoleum. I wondered to myself why all institutions feel so institutional. Then, when I was nearing the exit, I looked up. Outside, just past the glass doors, the cowboy lingered in the moonlight. I slowed my gait to savor the moment. It was my first real chance to put eyes on him without him noticing. Holy hot sauce, he was a choice cut of beef if I ever saw one. That boy got buns, hun. As if he could feel my eyes on him, he turned in my direction. He seemed uncomfortable. He was either nervous or he had to pee.

When I approached the door, he held it for me. Then he awkwardly blurted, "Hey, this might sound weird—it feels a little weird—but are you okay getting to your car in the dark?"

Was he worried about me? That was a little bit cute. Okay a lot, that was hot. I couldn't help flirting just a little. "I think so. Unless you're dangerous. Are you dangerous?"

It was cold and he exhaled a cloud of smoky air. His voice dropped an octave when he said, "Maybe."

I nervously laughed and then looked in my purse for my keys before saying, "So, does the serial killer thing work for you?"

"It can get kinda messy," he joked back. He paused briefly before dropping any dark pretense he'd been able to conjure. "No, sorry. I can't even make jokes about this. I didn't get the killer gene. I'm a cowboy who can't eat meat. I've never killed anything." Another pause. "I mean, for you, I might, but..." He let his words trail off and we just stood there looking in each other's eyes. His were oozy chocolate and I was swimming in them.

He was a funny mix of rugged man and awkward personality that I found almost completely irresistible. But I wasn't looking for attraction or even a tumble in the hay right now. I was on a mission to find me, to get secure in my own skin, and goofy, sexy, cowboy Morgan would be a big fat distraction from that, so it was time to head on home.

Shattering the eye contact, I looked toward my car and said, "Well, off I go."

"No to the escort then?" he asked.

"I'm good." I shrugged.

"You mind if I just stand here and make sure you get off okay?"

"It's a free country," I offered, already on the move.

To my back, he hollered, "I'm Luke, by the way."

"Maddie," I called back without turning around.

"Nice to meet you, Maddie," he said into the darkness punctuated by big overhead fluorescent parking lot lights.

I lifted my hand in a wave, my back still turned. I wasn't looking back. I didn't want to give him any ideas.

"Thank you for tonight, Maddie. You were exquisite."

I whipped around to see if he was joking. He didn't sound like he was, but no one had ever called me exquisite before. Nope, dead serious. And just like that, I found myself smiling and walking backwards like an idiot.

Nice moves, Madison. Way to stand your ground.

3

LUKE

The weekend after I first met Madison, Cody, Wyatt, and I ate lunch at Hazel's cafe in downtown Conway. When we finished eating, Cody stepped out onto the sidewalk and said, "I've been meaning to get a haircut, y'all mind?"

"Sounds good," Wyatt concurred.

I didn't need a haircut but I was happy to hang out with them, so all three of us walked half a block from Hazel's cafe to Delores' beauty shop. The shop was a little three-chair salon with a shampoo station behind a screen. There was also one of those hair drying bays, where little old gray-haired biddies in curlers spread town gossip. Delores was a forty-year-old single mom, who was fun and just an all-around kind woman. When you lived in Conway, she was the lady who cut your hair unless your mom did. Since our mom died, Delores took on the mantle for Morgan family grooming. There was a spell where our sister tried to do the job, but we started spooking the cattle so that didn't last.

As brothers tend to do, we were rowdy and goofing on each other as we walked through the door of the shop. I heard the tinkle of the bells on the door, and then I looked up, expecting Delores' *"Howdy,"* but instead, I got an eyeful of Maddie's baby blues.

She smiled warmly and said, "Hey, cowboy."

I panicked. I didn't want my brothers to know about my secret. I felt my eyes go wide. Moving as subtly as possible, I shook my head and mouthed the word, "No."

Maddie's reaction was visceral. I watched the color drain from her face and tension tightened her shoulders and jaw.

Cody stepped forward. "Hello there," he whistled. He was a dead man. "You are not Delores."

Wyatt decided he wanted me to kill him too by stepping in front of Cody and cooing, "Pay no heed to this little baby peacock. I'm Wyatt."

I couldn't control myself, I growled, "Both of you. Sit down." Searching behind Maddie with my eyes, I hollered, "Delores, Wyatt and Cody need their hair cut!"

"That's my job," Maddie said. "Who would like to go first?"

Cody moved to volunteer, but I stepped in front of him. "Me. I'll go."

Delores finally appeared, coming out of the bathroom and drying her hands with a paper towel. "Well, howdy," she exclaimed. Then she turned to Maddie. "Did they introduce themselves? These are the Morgan brothers."

Maddie forced a smile. "I'm pretty sure they were getting around to it."

Nodding toward Maddie, Delores said, "This is Madison, but she goes by Maddie. She's my new partner and a damn good stylist."

I offered Maddie my hand. "I'm Luke."

She rebuked the offer of my hand, turning toward the shampoo station. "Follow me."

Cody shouted across the room, "I thought you weren't getting a haircut?"

Without looking back, I flipped him the bird and kept walking.

When we got behind the screen, Maddie threw a smock at me and commanded me to, "Sit."

I did what I was told. She tucked a towel behind my head without touching me or saying a word. I could hear her fooling around with the water when she said, "Lean back."

The anticipation of her hands running through my hair had me at half-mast.

Lulled by my own thoughts, I relaxed into the rush of water. It was fucking freezing. I jumped two feet in the air. "What the f—"

Standing there with her arms crossed over her spectacular bosom, Maddie snickered, "Oops, my bad."

I think she expected me to walk away. Instead, I took a deep breath and sat back down. Once my head fell backward, she hit me with a second arctic shot across my brow. I didn't move a muscle. Dismayed by my persistence, she harrumphed and opened the hot water valve so that the temperature warmed up.

Sweet baby Jesus, when her fingers made contact with my scalp, it took every manly bone in my body not to audibly moan. Her hands rubbing circles on my skull was one of the most intense pleasures of my life. Hard as nails, it was all I could do not to bust my nut. In an attempt to resume hostilities, Maddie tugged roughly at the ends of my long blond locks. Her efforts totally backfired. It was like she sprinkled Miracle-Gro across my crotch. My dick, which I would have sworn was as big as it could possibly get, swelled. It was like a third person entered the room, made known by the very visible rise in my Wranglers.

"Should I turn the cold water back on?" Maddie asked.

It was a joke, which I guess was better than her anger, but I was pretty sure she was still pissed. There was no way I could explain myself. Cody and Wyatt could definitely hear us. I didn't really even want them to know I was sporting King Kong, but I certainly wasn't ashamed of how Maddie affected me. It was glorious.

With a wink, I said the only thing I could. "I'm good, thanks."

She rolled her eyes, leaving me to wrap up my own hair and adjust my situation, while she moved on to her chair.

Once I was seated, she combed out my hair and asked, "What are we doing? Buzz cut?"

I'm not sure about all long-haired men, but my hair was insanely important to me. There was one time when I was a teenager that Wyatt put Nair in my shampoo. It was bad. I looked like one of those hairless cats. So, threatening my tresses helped convince my one-eyed monster that retreating back into his cave was a viable option.

I pleaded with my eyes while trying to maintain my masculinity. "Just a trim, please."

Recognizing my fear, she bit out, "Don't worry. I'm a professional."

After that, she didn't talk much, just directions to turn this way and that so that she could do her job. I watched her in the mirror. Just like in class, I couldn't take my eyes off her, mesmerized by her beauty. But it was also fun to watch her work. I could tell by her focus that cutting hair wasn't perfunctory for Maddie. It was her art. She had a vision, and each snip was a step toward the image in her mind.

Both Wyatt and Cody were done before Maddie let me out of her chair. They were lingering, stalking around like hungry vultures.

Standing at the register, Delores asked, "One bill or three, boys?"

Cody poked the bear. "Oh, I'm pretty sure Luke is paying for me and Wyatt, considering he kept us from talking to Maddie, the blue-haired beauty."

"I know someone who could write that song." Wyatt was referencing Bill's rock star ex-girlfriend's first hit, "Blue Eyed Beau." "You interested in being serenaded, Maddie?"

I was generally a gentle guy, but in this case, I didn't want either of these idiots thinking they had even a glimmer of a chance with my girl. I pulled out my wallet, handed Delores eighty bucks, and addressing my brothers, said, "Not now. Not ever." Then I turned to Maddie. Again, I tried to convey my apology with my eyes. "It was lovely to meet you. I truly hope to see you again soon." I pulled a ten out of my wallet and tried to give it to her.

She threw a towel over her shoulder and said, "I'll pass."

And then she spun on her heel and I watched her sweet ass walk away.

Shit.

4

MADDIE

I threw the broom and dustpan in the supply closet with a little too much force and it clattered noisily. *Damn it.* It was four o'clock on Tuesday night and Delores and I were cleaning up the salon. I was modeling in the art class in a couple of hours and I wasn't happy about it.

From behind me, Delores questioned, "What is up with you today?"

"Nothing," I growled.

"Yeah, sure, and the Pope's bar mitzvah is next weekend."

"It's really nothing. You know that thing I am doing at the college?"

Delores giggled like a schoolboy who just heard someone say boobies. "Your risqué

empowerment project?" she joked.

"Yes," I rolled my eyes. "My art modeling. Thing is, Luke Morgan is in the class."

"Luke Morgan, Luke Morgan?"

I nodded confirmation.

Delores cackled. Her whole body shook and she rocked forward, her hair falling over her face. I took a deep breath and tried not to be annoyed that she was laughing at my life. Once she regained her composure, she said, "Well, the whole it's-far-enough-from-my-backyard plan backfired." She paused for a minute and I could see the wheels turning in her head. "Wait a minute, then you already knew him when the Morgan brothers came in over the weekend?"

I nodded again, letting her work it out for herself.

"Did he pretend he didn't know you?" It was a rhetorical question. "That's weird."

A couple of days ago, when he first walked into the shop, my heart leapt. It was just instinctual; I was so happy to see him. Happier than I would have expected. And then when he caged up, I felt terrible. Obviously, he thought that taking my clothes off and modeling for an art class was not respectable. He was either embarrassed for me that I was an art model or he didn't want his brothers to think I was a whore. And even worse, he didn't want his brothers to flirt with or date me because he thought of me as dirty. Then he was so turned on by me touching him, and for a second, that felt exciting, but when the thought of it settled in, I was horrified. I was like porn for him, a sex object. I was modeling in this class because I wanted to feel people honoring my body as a thing of beauty, so that I could feel that beauty as my own empowerment, not to be fodder for some jerk's spank bank.

I didn't say all that to Delores. "I guess he didn't want his brothers to know I'm a nude model."

"Oh, honey, around here, the gossip moves fast; he might have been trying to keep that under wraps for you. Wyatt and Cody are wild ones. They might get the wrong idea," she reasoned.

"I guess, maybe. He seemed a little intense about it," I grumped. Luke seemed like he was close to his brothers. After they left the other day, Delores mentioned that there were four of them and a sister too. If this bullshit with him hiding my modeling hadn't happened, that would be another reason for me to stay away from him. Boys with big families tended to want big families, and I could never offer him that.

"If you ask me, you seem awfully moody about one interaction with Luke Morgan."

Ugh, I hated and loved insightful people like Delores. It was so hard to keep them from nosing in your business. "We might have had a connection for a minute, but it was obviously nothing."

"Obviously."

I got to the meat of the issue. "I feel super weird about modeling in front of him tonight."

"Why?"

"I don't know. I just feel like he thinks it's something I should be ashamed of and that makes it totally not empowering." I kept it to myself that Luke got a giant erection when I touched him. I just didn't know what to do with that information for a number of reasons. First, even through his pants, I could tell that was the thickest, longest hose I had ever seen, and I was intrigued. Second, I had this visceral physical reaction to everything about Luke Morgan, and touching his hair had made me as wet as he was hard. Third, I was really mad at myself for feeling sexually drawn (pun intended) to a dude that made me feel dirty. I wasn't sharing any of that with Delores; it was just too personal.

"Fuck him. If he doesn't like it," Delores said.

Oh, he liked it.

I GOT to Fletcher Community College with no time to spare. I didn't want to talk to Luke at all. I stopped in the bathroom near the class, changed into my nude bra and panties, and put on my brand-new kimono, which I totally got on Amazon. Luke was already in his seat when I entered the room. I wondered if he showed up early because he was hoping to talk to me. Professor Rufus seemed downright flustered by my on-time arrival.

"Madeline, if you could arrive a few minutes early, it would do wonders for my nerves," he said.

Still not my name. I wasn't in the mood to please anyone, so I snapped, "I'll think about it." Then I climbed up to my chair in the center of the room, took off my kimono, sat down, and waited for Rufus to drape me. I didn't look at Luke. Didn't acknowledge him one bit. The week earlier, I was draped before the students came into the classroom. Dropping my kimono in front of them, in front of Luke, felt like I was being defiant. I wanted to be brazen, to metaphorically say, *"You don't like it that I'm getting naked in front of a room full of people. Well, too bad, mister."*

It worked for like a minute.

But as the room quieted down, the only sound the scratch of pencils on paper, my bravado slipped. Like the week before, I felt his eyes on me, caressing me, devouring me with that same insatiable hunger. Only this time, knowing that he didn't respect me made it feel wrong. Instead of feeling the embodiment and beauty I expected to feel, I felt the opposite of the bodily empowerment I was seeking. I felt shame.

Unlike the week before, all the eyes on me were totally overwhelming. Every glance felt like a judgment. I wanted to jump up and run from the room, but that wasn't the job. I took quiet breaths through my nose and tried to quell the storm inside my chest. I would get through this. And if I couldn't come back next week, then that would be okay. Or maybe I'd tell Luke not to come back. Maybe there was still some way to salvage this situation and get what I wanted and needed from this experience. I'd find a solution. I was strong and could get through anything. Even this. But for certain, no matter what, no matter how gross or horrible I felt, I wasn't going to cry in this room. I wouldn't give him the satisfaction of reveling in my shame.

I got to class even earlier than usual because I wanted the opportunity to talk to Maddie and explain how I acted in the salon. I figured that she would get to the class early too because she had to be draped, but when I arrived, she wasn't there. Anthony was already sitting at his easel. Over the course of the semester, we had developed a camaraderie. He was a good guy. He liked to talk, and I'd learned a lot about him during the first few weeks of class. He was the youngest of five siblings and lived in one house with four generations of family. Talking to Anthony reminded me of hanging out with Cody. We had things in common, but he always felt like a kid to me.

As I got settled, Anthony teasingly said, "Dude, heads up, we're still drawing the blue girl. So maybe take this time to get your head on straight?"

With Maddie on my mind, I started chatting. "I actually ran into her this weekend."

"Blue?"

I didn't like him referring to her at all, let alone by a silly nickname, "Her name is Maddie, Anthony. She's a person, not just an object for you to draw."

He threw his hands up in gentle defense. "Whoa, down boy. I'm just a bad listener, not an ass. I missed her name. And, come on, her defining characteristic is certainly that mane of blue, is it not?"

I shrugged dreamily. "It's pretty freakin' gorgeous."

"No offense, dude, but I wouldn't have pegged you as a guy into a girl with an alternative vibe. It's kinda like pairing a pony with a peacock."

I smiled. "Anthony, I didn't know you thought my colorful tail was so sexy."

He shook his head. "I would make a pea-cock joke, but you're a big dude. Not looking to ruffle your feathers."

I was smiling to myself, thinking he was a quick-witted kid, when Maddie walked into the room. She showed up right on time, so I didn't get a chance to speak to her. She wore a floral kimono and had her hair pulled up in a loose bun at the nape of her neck. Even though I knew she was going to model, I was startled when she dropped her robe in front of the class. The irrational beast inside of me wanted to march up to her and cover her up like an idiot dad in a sitcom about his developing daughter. Maddie brought out a part of me that I didn't even know existed—this growling caveman that constantly wanted to claim her as mine and throw her over my shoulder.

As usual, she was painfully beautiful. For a second, I was consumed by the sight of her. My heart raced. My dick rose. But before my libido totally took over, warning bells blared in my brain. I stopped looking and I started to really watch her. Maddie was not okay. She wouldn't look my way. I could feel her discomfort from across the room. She was trembling with the need to cry. What the hell was going on? The Maddie I met the week before—glorious and confident— was nowhere to be found. Everything inside of me wilted. I couldn't draw at all. I wanted to scream at all the people in the room, *Get the fuck out.* Or pick her up and carry her away and cradle her to my chest until she wasn't hurting anymore. But instead, I just sat there, counting the minutes, looking at her trembling jaw, wondering how I could fix what was happening in front of me.

When class was over, Maddie jumped up, grabbed her kimono, and ran. I was hot on her heels. She made a beeline for the ladies' room. I hesitated at the door for a second, but when I heard crying, I couldn't help myself. I had to go in.

As I plowed through the two sets of doors that protected the inner sanctum of the ladies' room, the gentleman in me insisted on a disclaimer. "Listen up, I don't mean any offense, but man coming in," I hollered.

What they say about the women's bathroom was true. It didn't smell nearly as bad as the men's room, but it was still ugly. Teal and burnt-orange tiles, tan stalls, and Maddie leaning on a sink, black smears of mascara running down her cheeks. I went across to her but stopped when she wept, "Is it not enough that you made me feel dirty in there? You need to fucking accost me in the ladies' room?"

Whoa. What was happening here? Was I somehow lecherous when I looked at her? Honestly, I felt a little lecherous when I looked at her. I stayed very still. Not sure what to say. I decided it was best to ask. I kept my tone calm and even, even though I was scared that I had somehow wrecked us before we'd begun. "Okay, I'm a little lost. I see that you are very upset, and I want to understand. Please, Maddie, tell me what I did? If you can explain it to me, I promise I won't do it again."

She was crying hard, sniffling and struggling to catch her breath. After a few messy moments, she regained her composure and her sadness transformed into rage. "Really? You don't know what you did? You come into my shop so embarrassed of me that you don't want your brothers to know we know each other and you don't want them interested in me. Why? Because I'm dirty?"

I stuttered. It never occurred to me that she would assume that I was embarrassed of her. Why would anyone be embarrassed of Maddie? She was spectacular. She didn't give me a chance to speak.

"And what kind of man does that make you? You're embarrassed that I take my clothes off for art, but looking at me makes you fucking hard as steel. I guess you're a fucking perv who gets off on sluts, huh?"

That was enough of that. I had something to say now. "Stop."

"You don't get to—"

I interrupted her, my voice forceful, bordering on a full-blown yell. "Stop it. I won't listen to you talk about yourself like that. You're amazing. You're brave and willful and exceptional. I love that you model in this art class even though I want to beg the others not to look because I'm jealous. I don't want my brothers hitting on you because I want you for myself, and the only person who should feel shame about this art class is me because I'm too scared to tell my family that I think I'm an artist, not just a rancher, so I'm hiding this class from them."

Maddie looked at me with wonder, her mouth hanging open. Behind me, the bathroom door opened and my weasley professor sternly said, "Mr. Morgan, this is the ladies' room. Is everything okay in here, Madeline?"

A fire still burning in my chest, I turned to him and spat, "Listen up, her name is freaking Madison. Not Madeline. *Mad-i-son*. You got it?"

Maddie came up behind me and pressed her hand to the small of my back. All the angry energy slipped away at her touch. She spoke to Prof. Douche Canoe, her voice soft and no longer weighed down with sadness. "Everything is fine, Rufus. Just a misunderstanding."

Rufus was a perfect name for that guy.

His face red with embarrassment from my attack, Rufus clamored to reestablish his authority. "Very well. Mr. Morgan, you still are not allowed in the ladies' room." He held the door open and signaled for me to leave.

Maddie dropped her hand from my back to my palm and squeezed. "Wait for me outside?"

I nodded and strutted past Rufus, heading straight for her car. It didn't take very long for Maddie to push through the building doors. I watched her walking toward me; her blue hair was loose now and she was wearing a yellow knit cap. She looked sweet, like a girl ready to play in the snow. I wanted to build a snowman with her. You know that feeling? When you totally have the hots for someone, but you also just want to have fun with them, the kind of fun you had when you were a kid. Hearty, ruddy-cheeked, playful, laugh-filled fun.

When she got close enough for me to hear her, she said, "I feel like an idiot."

That was to be expected but not necessary. "Don't. It was my fault."

She didn't say anything.

I took her fingers in mine and briefly looked down to see the contrast of her feminine hand in my callused one. Then I looked back into her eyes. "I'm sorry you felt all those things."

She swallowed, looked away, and sadness crossed her face again. "I have to wonder why, right? That was quite a story I built up in my head." She paused, and I used my hand to turn her face back to me. "For the record, I'm not a fucking psycho," she said.

"Well, some people think I'm a serial killer, so..."

"You do have that look about you," she flirted. She was close now. Close enough that I could feel the warmth of her body in my space.

My voice got husky and deep with my desire. "I wanna take you out, Maddie."

She got closer. "Okay," she answered, her breath on my lips. Fuck, I wanted to kiss her so badly. I wanted to slam her against the side of her car, wrap her legs around my waist, and make her come. But moments ago, I'd made her feel used. So, instead, I pulled her to me, hugged her against me so that we were cheek to cheek, and whispered in her ear, "I want to kiss you. And I'm going to kiss you, but when I kiss you, Maddie, you won't question what my intentions are."

6

MADDIE

"What am I doing?" I asked Mr. Wiggles, my cat.

Mr. Wiggles, Wigs for short, was gray with icy eyes and a blue collar. We were into blue in our house. He perched beside me on the bathroom sink as I examined myself in the mirror. Luke was due to arrive soon and I was still in my bra and underwear. I'd been having the age-old underwear argument with myself. Wear a matching set or go with granny panties? This man had me all tied up in knots. Normally, I wouldn't even consider a matching set on a first date, but dating Luke felt different than any man before him. Considering he'd basically already seen me naked and come so close to kissing me, I decided on the matching set.

"Don't look at me like that," I scolded Wigs. "You're not my keeper."

I hadn't been on a date in a while. I didn't even mean to be going on one now. I knew it was a bad idea, but there was something inescapable about my connection to Luke. Maybe it was just hormones. For the record, all he had to do was show up and I was reeling. Luke Morgan was the real deal, an honest to goodness panty dropper. My connection to him kept overruling my sanity. For the first time in my life, I looked at a man and thought maybe I could love someone and he could love me. It was ridiculous, I hardly knew him. But when I was standing next to him, it felt like we could be something. Only, we couldn't be. For me, Luke was a fling at best. There's no way I was in his future once he realized what I couldn't offer him. But there was something about being near him that I couldn't deny myself. This was my year of self-exploration, right? So maybe my body love journey needed to include a sweateringly hot cowboy lovin' on my body. Why not? Seemed perfectly rational to me.

I pulled my favorite navy-blue velvet top from my closet. It had a sweetheart neckline that accentuated my assets. There was no denying I had boobs—and the thing about big boobs was that showing a little cleavage was always more flattering than covering them up. Fully covered boobs looked trapped. Also, the velvet top was a perfect piece of clothing. It made me feel sexy but not uncomfortable, and it was dressy without being overstated. I paired it with black skinny jeans and red cowboy boots. I was from Montana, after all. Keeping makeup to a minimum, I used only mascara and lip gloss, but spent way too much time on my hair. I always spent too much time on my hair. I wore it down in loose waves. The end result was sexy—not too dressy, not too casual, just right.

Eventually, I was ready, standing in the middle of my living room, not wanting to sit and wrinkle my first impression but also desperately wanting to sit because I literally didn't know what to do with myself while I waited for him to arrive. Unable to find a solution, I just stood there, far enough away from the door that he would think I was doing something when he rang because he would hear the sound of my boots on the wood floor when I walked up to answer the bell. It didn't take very long. He was perfectly on time. It was respectful to be on time for a date. It proved you wanted to be there.

At the sound of the doorbell, a cacophony of butterflies took flight in my chest. How could I be nervous to see a man I already knew, one who had made it perfectly clear that he was interested in me? God, I was so into him. I took a quick breath and pulled the door open. I half expected him to be leaning on the doorframe, cocky like a James Dean-esque character from a movie with fifties greasers, but he wasn't. He was standing a healthy distance away from me, which gave me the opportunity to check out what his A-game looked like, and it looked good. He was still in his Wranglers, but he topped them with a crisp white Oxford shirt, a black leather belt, and boots. He'd left his hat at home and pulled his shiny blond hair back into a slightly messy but perfectly executed knot. He'd also trimmed his dark beard close. Man, I could really appreciate a man who cared about grooming his hair.

Realizing I'd been stunned into silence by his good looks, I said, "Hi." It came out bashful.

"Hi," he said back, resonantly. He had his hands pushed deep into his pockets. We stood there for another beat. Then he spoke. "You look beautiful, Maddie."

I looked down and played the game, making a series of faces and gestures like *oh really, this old thing,* when we all knew I spent the entire day figuring out what I was going to wear. Then I said "Thank you. You don't look half bad yourself."

He didn't seem to move, just stood there looking into my eyes, and I wondered if I should invite him in. Mr. Wiggles rubbed up on my leg and purred. Luke looked down, then crouched to pet my cat. I'm not gonna lie, Mr. Wiggles is a slut. He'll rub up on anyone.

Luke looked up at me. "Name?"

"Mr. Wiggles," I answered.

He chuckled to himself. "Fitting. I'll take good care of your girl tonight, Wigs. Promise to bring her back to you in one piece. Okay?"

See, totally Wigs for short.

———

BY THE TIME we got to the restaurant, I was flush and over-heating. Luke smelled amazing. I caught my first whiff as he opened his truck door for me. His scent was like musk and earth, a woodsy clean man smell. He put his hand on my waist as I climbed into the truck and the imprint of his touch singed my skin. I could feel the echo of his fingertips the entire drive. Inside the cab, his smell intensified. I was drunk from it, desperate to crawl onto his lap and bury my nose in the nape of his neck. I could see the strength in his thick thighs every time he pressed the accelerator. Holy ravioli, Batman, I was like a dog in heat.

He drove us to Sundancer, which was the best restaurant in town. He held my hand as we walked in and kept holding it as the hostess greeted us.

"Hi, Luke," she said. She was a little blond thing, couldn't have been more than fifteen, but I irrationally hated that he knew her. I reminded myself that Conway was small. Everyone knew everyone. It was something I liked. He spoke to her like the kid that she was.

"Nice to see you, Carly. How's your dad?" He squeezed my hand.

"Nosy and completely irrational." She rolled her eyes. "He won't let me go on a date with Curtis."

"Well, maybe that's because Curtis is a little old for you?" he suggested.

"Whatever." She pursed her lips. "Two?"

"Yes, can we have a booth please?"

Carly grabbed two menus and started walking. We followed. Luke leaned over and whispered in my ear. "Curtis is like twenty-five. Maybe older."

I smiled. He didn't want me to feel left out. I'd never been to Sundancer before. The restaurant was dark and felt like a British duke's library, lots of glowing brass fixtures and wood molding. The tables had white tablecloths and they were candlelit. It was fancy, small-town fancy, but fancy all the same. The booth Carly brought us to was a circular one. Seeing this, I realized he wanted to sit next to me. I slipped into the booth on one side, scooting toward the middle and he did the same. Carly handed us our menus. Then she was gone.

"Do you mind?" he asked, referencing the booth and our closeness.

I shook my head. "No."

"I planned it," he said guiltily. "I dreamed about it all day actually. Being this close to you all through dinner."

I smiled. I loved this about him. This painful need to be honest. "It's good," I said. "I like being close to you too." I felt him press his thigh against mine, and he plastered a goofy toothy smile on his face.

"Whatever makes you happy, ma'am," he said.

I laughed at him. "Okay, so we've figured out we like to touch each other. How about we figure out if we're well suited? Tell me something about yourself."

He leaned his elbow against the table and turned his torso so he was facing me just a bit more. "Let's see, I'm a rancher. Second oldest of the Morgan boys. There are four of us. You met Wyatt and Cody. My older brother is Bill. I've got a sister too, Sarah. My momma passed when I was fifteen. My pop still runs the ranch, even though Bill acts like it's his."

I knew he was a family man. I tried not to get stuck on that and just went where he led me. "That sounds contentious. Do you not get along with Bill?"

"No, I get along with Bill just fine. He's just a grumpy guy."

"Like that's his schtick, grumpy all the time? Is there a reason?"

Luke bit his lip. There was something he wanted to say but didn't.

"What?" I asked.

"You're not from here so you're gonna think I'm lying."

I needled him with my elbow. "Come on, now I'm curious."

"Bill made a mistake with a girl a while back."

"That's not so unbelievable," I argued.

"The girl was Kat Bennett. She grew up in Conway."

The only Kat Bennett I knew was a songwriter, an international superstar, the kind of musical success that was a household name.

"Like *the* Kat Bennett? The platinum records, Grammy-winning Kat Bennett?"

"Yeah," he nodded. "That's the one."

I scoffed. "Sounds like a pretty big mistake."

"She was our neighbor growing up," he said. "I'd say we're like family but it's a long story. Bill and she were in love... well, always. And then she went off and got famous and I'm not sure what happened to him. Part of me thinks they'll figure it out sooner or later, and we will be family again, but they're going on ten years of not talking. It's really sad."

"You think he still loves her?" I asked.

"I think they still love each other. They're just both stubborn and pigheaded. Always have been."

It was kinda romantic. "What is she like?"

"She's just Kat. She's funny and friendly and cool. I've known her since I was in diapers. Her house is a stone's throw from my front door. She loved my brother. She played

guitar with my sister. We talked about stuff and we were
friends. Also, she sings really well," he joked.

I laughed. Then I shifted gears. "I'm sorry about your mom."

"Thank you. It was a long time ago but I still miss her. You
want to see a picture?"

I nodded. I thought he would pull out his phone, but he
pulled out his wallet and took a tattered old photo from its
folds. The image wasn't just his mother. It was his whole
family. But it wasn't a portrait. It was a candid shot. His
mother was standing behind the older three boys who were
elementary-aged and holding two toddlers, one with
pigtails. Everyone was smiling and covered in red paint,
including his mom. Again, I was reminded that family
mattered to him, enough that he kept a photo of them with
him all the time.

"We painted the barn," he explained. "We wanted to help
my dad, only, we did a terrible job and mostly painted each
other."

"She's pretty," I offered. "And she looks kind."

"She was a great mom," he said wistfully. He took the photo
back and returned it to his wallet. "What about you?" he
asked. "What's your story?"

I felt obligated to explain my family. There was no way to
avoid it after he'd basically just described himself by giving
me a family tree.

I sighed. "My parents were not that nice. I don't speak to
them anymore."

I turned to examine his eyes, expecting to find pity there, but he wasn't pitying me. He looked curious more than anything. "Do you want to tell me more?" he asked gently. "You don't have to. But I'd like to know. I'd like to get you, and I think where we come from plays a role in who we are."

I was surprised to find that I wanted to tell him. So I did. "They weren't physically abusive or anything. But they ripped me of my self-esteem." I prided myself on talking openly about the history of my eating disorder and I didn't see a reason to stop that now. "I managed their cruelty by developing an eating disorder. I don't know how much you know about anorexia and bulimia, but people think they are beauty disorders, when they are really about control. Controlling my body helped me feel secure in a place where I was treated unkindly. It's more complicated than that but I worked hard to put it behind me. When I was eighteen, I got a job at a restaurant and I was lucky enough to meet a woman named Claire, who helped me."

"How did she help?" he asked. He was really listening.

"She helped me move out of my parents' house. Gave me somewhere to stay, rent-free, so I could afford my therapist. And then let me continue to stay with her when I decided to go to cosmetology school. Claire is my family. She's the person who cared for me and the person I cared for the most in my life."

"Where is she now? Can I meet her?" He smiled.

I shrugged and flirted. "If you play your cards right."

"Do you worry that you'll relapse?" he asked. It was a fair question, but he clarified anyway. "Just to be clear, I'm not scared that you have an eating disorder in your past. We all have baggage. I mean, as you know, I'm not brave enough to tell my brothers I'm an artist. Not that that's the same." He rolled his eyes at himself. "I'm trying to say, I'm just curious how you feel about it."

"My parents were my trigger. As long as they're nowhere near me, I don't worry about having an eating disorder."

"I'd say that was sort of sad, but it sounds like they aren't worth knowing. And you made a new family."

I did. Claire was my family.

He reached for my hand under the table and I threaded my fingers with his. The waiter came over. We ordered dinner and a bottle of wine. I got the trout and Luke had some creamy pasta dish, reminding me that he was a vegetarian.

I tore a hunk of bread off the loaf in the basket that the waiter left behind and asked, "So, how does a cowboy wind up only eating sprouts?"

He shrugged. "Hypocrite, I guess. I'm just a bleeding heart. I can't kill 'em, so I can't eat 'em. But I still make a living off them. It's really an atrocity." He laughed.

I laughed too.

He spoke with such passion. "How can anyone take me seriously? My brothers call me Patty. Short for hamburger patty. It's just ludicrous."

"They're tough on you," I suggested.

"Sometimes." He shrugged. "Honestly, I think I'm tough on me. The teasing is all in good fun and it doesn't always bother me, but I don't want to disappoint them, ya know? We run this ranch together. And we really support each other. I just don't want them to feel like they can't count on me, like the ranch doesn't matter to me..."

He was talking seriously. Thinking deeply about his relationship with his brothers, something that he had clearly identified to me as important to him and also complicated, so while he spoke, I instinctually rested my hand on his knee to comfort him. But as soon as I touched him, he stopped speaking. He licked his lips and pulled a tight breath through his nose. It took me a second but I realized my hand on his knee was a catalyst. My touch turned him on, so much that he lost his train of thought.

Not trying to be slut-shaming, to each their own, but I didn't normally do the kind of thing I did next, yet with Luke, something came over me. I slid my hand higher and felt his thigh muscle tighten under my fingers. I looked up into his eyes and watched his Adam's apple bob as he gulped in anticipation. He certainly didn't seem horrified. I moved higher. He sucked in another breath. And then, he was in my hand, thick and hard under the denim of his jeans. I made a sound, a low hum of appreciation, an animalistic sound, announcing my own excitement. He got harder.

Through gritted teeth, he joked, "Check, please."

I laughed and released him, pulling up my hands to cover my face. "Oh my God," I said, hiding behind my palms. "I can't believe I just did that." I was pretty sure I was blushing from head to toe. I peeked out from between my fingers to look at him.

He had a cocky grin on his face as he threw his arms behind him on the back of the booth and flopped his legs open so that his knee crashed into mine. "Not complaining," he quipped. He turned toward me, dipped down, and nibbled on my ear, sending shivers down my spine. Then he dropped his hand to my knee before he breathed out, "Do I turn you on too, Maddie?"

Yes. So much yes.

7

LUKE

Maddie's chest rose and fell in heavy pants as I pressed into her side, dragging my fingertips up her thigh like she had done to me. I kept trying to remind myself to slow down, that I hadn't even kissed her yet, but Maddie made me so hungry. When she opened the door to her house, I was so taken aback by her beauty that I almost couldn't form words, and now, as she told me details about her life, I just wanted more. I wanted to know every story. What was her favorite color? What were her dreams? Did she want kids? How did she take her coffee? I wanted all the details. I wanted to know her inside and out. I'd literally never felt this drive about anyone. I was almost jealous of my brother, Bill, that he grew up right next to the woman of his dreams so he always knew her. I had missed so much already.

Our waiter, Jesse Christensen, brought over our entrees, and his eyes went a little wide when he saw how close I was to Maddie. Jesse wasn't a particularly chatty guy, but we got in a fight in elementary school, and in a small town, you're never quite certain who's holding a grudge. I really didn't want Conway talking smack about Maddie, so I protected her honor from Jesse's prying eyes and pulled back a touch. When he walked away, I turned to Maddie, worried that she might have feelings of rejection like she did in the salon. She didn't seem offended. Instead, there was the rosy blush of embarrassment across the apple of her cheeks.

"We are so in public," she said as if we had both forgotten.

"Sadly true," I teased and she smacked my arm.

I picked up my fork and took a bite of my pasta. It was good. It had been a long time since I ate dinner in a restaurant. If I wasn't eating at the ranch, I usually just grabbed a meal out of my freezer. Maddie also took a bite of her trout, closing her eyes as she savored the flavors.

"Good?" I asked.

She opened her eyes and nodded. "Delicious. You want a bite? Wait, do you eat fish?"

"I mean, not that often. I really just don't eat farm animals. If I had to raise one, I don't eat it. I don't eat goldfish either."

"I'm guessing you never had a pet trout," she joked.

"No, never."

"Then you should taste this. It's incredible." She lifted her fork to my mouth. Sharing food with a woman was intimate. It just was. Putting my lips around Maddie's fork had me thinking of other things. Dirty things, but I kept it together, for now. The fish was tender, and the sauce was the perfect balance of lemon and creamy. It was really good. She was right.

"Delectable. Do you want to taste mine?" I asked.

She nodded. I loaded up my fork for her. Maddie's lips closing around my fork was actually physically painful. I groaned. It was an instinctual reaction; I couldn't have contained it if I wanted to.

"Maybe we should skip dessert," she said. I so wanted that, but I wasn't going to let her miss the cheesecake.

"We can't," I grumbled.

She seemed surprised but not adverse. "Why not?"

"It's the best part of this restaurant. They have huckleberry cheesecake brought up from Elle's Belles bakery in Bozeman."

"I want to be able to tell you that I don't like cheesecake, but I really like cheesecake."

I swung my fist across my body like gosh darn it. I had to get my head out of her pants. Honesty was always my policy, and so far, she didn't seem to mind. "I kind of have a one-track mind right now." I waggled my eyebrows as a silent innuendo. "Talk to me, distract me from my naughty thoughts."

She blushed again. "Tell me more about you. How long have you been an artist?"

"Always," I said. "The first time I remember drawing, it was with the ash from a campfire. I used to collect the cooled embers. I kept them in a tin and kept the tin in my saddle-bag. I drew on anything: lined paper, rocks, the side of the barn. Mostly, I sketched scenes from our ranch. A lot of nature, but sometimes the animals or my siblings. My mom used to nag me because there was always charcoal all over my clothes. I think I was ten when she gave me my first set of real charcoal pencils and a sketchbook. I took art in high school, but this is my first real drawing class, and the first time I've drawn a live model." I winked at her, took a bite of food, then asked, "What about you? How did you start modeling for artists?"

She swallowed the food in her mouth and then said, "Actually, this is the first time I've ever modeled."

"Really?" I asked. "You seem so natural up there. What made you want to try it?"

"I made a body love resolution this year. I wanted to push myself to grow my relationship with my body, learn to like it more, and feel beautiful in my skin."

Flabbergasted, I choked on my food. It was hard for me to imagine that Maddie felt anything but love for her body since I was enthralled by it.

She patted my back, giggling. "You okay?"

I couldn't help but be cocky. "Anytime you need reassurance that your body is worth loving, I am your guy."

She shook her head, smiling. I made her happy and I liked it.

I PUSHED the door open and the cool evening air rushed in. I held it for her and she walked past me, tucking her scarf a little tighter around her neck as she said, "You were right. Missing the cheesecake would have been a sin unto itself."

She looked soft and beautiful in the moonlight. It was a perfect date, the best one of my entire life. She was silly and sexy and real. It seemed so crazy that I hadn't even kissed her yet. It was time to remedy that. I took her hand and we made the short walk to the passenger door of my truck. Before I could open the door, she leaned against it and bit the lower lip of her lush pink mouth. No time like the present.

I leaned in slowly, savoring the last seconds of anticipation. When I felt her breath on my lips, I couldn't control myself any longer. I took her face in my hands and crushed my mouth to hers. Quickly, we upgraded from a lip-lock to a tangle of tongues and teeth. She was sweet and savory at the same time, putting huckleberry cheesecake to shame. My hands slipped lower, pulling her body flush to mine. She shifted our weight so I was pressing her against the door of my truck. I could feel her breasts heaving against my chest. I was losing control.

I slowed the rhythm of my kisses, and with my forehead pressed against hers, I broke from her mouth and said, "We should..."

"...leave the parking lot," she finished, her voice all breathy and raw with need.

8

MADDIE

After our first kiss, I was having trouble keeping my hands off him. He helped me into his truck and then, with him on the ground and me in the passenger seat, we wound up making out again before we even got out of the parking lot. Then I found myself creeping across the cab to be closer to him and attacking his face at every red light. The guy behind us had to honk more than once to alert us that the traffic light was green. Luke seemed too good to be true. He was funny and sweet. He was attentive and interested. And he was so hot. For the record, habanero hot.

Luke appeared to be as taken with me as I was with him. Of course, there was a little part of me that was thinking, *he's a dude. You grabbed his dick in public. What dude wouldn't be into that? But...* he also seemed to care about my history and my passions. He even asked me what my favorite color was. Blue, duh. But also, why would he care what my favorite color was unless he really wanted to know me, like really. I wasn't used to letting people in. I wasn't used to people being interested in me. That was not one hundred percent true. I had a mane of blue hair. People looked at me, made assumptions that I was cool, and wanted me as their token alternative friend. But beyond that, I didn't often sit across the table from a man who wanted to know me. It was one thing to go on a date with him when I thought we were just having fun. But even though not being able to keep my hands off him was so fun, it was also starting to feel like more than just fun, for both of us.

When we pulled up in front of my house, he put his truck in park and I felt a little stymied. There was a big piece of me that was like, *Ahoy, sailor. Why don't you come inside and let me show you the pleasure dome?* But there was also this other piece of me that was freaking the fuck out. I was quiet, working on finding some appropriate balance in this situation. Like how did I explain myself? I couldn't just come out and say, *Hey, listen, I was so totally thinking we were headed toward dancing the forbidden polka, but you're so cool that I'm emotionally strung out and wishing my sixth-grade teacher were here to chaperone.* I didn't want it to end. I didn't want to go to bed with him and then wake up tomorrow and it was all over.

Luke spoke first. "Maddie? You okay?"

Shit, he was totally going to think I was crazy. I was practically humping him at red lights and now here we were in front of my house, a perfect place for making whoopie just steps away and I'd totally clammed up.

So far, he was always honest with me, so I figured I'd follow his lead. "I feel... nervous. I know I've been giving you gung ho take me right here, right now signals all night, but..."

I paused, trying to think of the most diplomatic way to get my point across.

"But now you feel like it's a little too much too fast?" he asked.

I nodded.

"That's okay, Maddie. I'm really enjoying sucking face." He was so silly, like me. I liked him so much. I wasn't ready for him to leave.

"So... I was thinking... You wanna come in, suck face, and maybe tweedle my dee?"

He didn't answer me. He just jumped out of the truck and ran for the door, bouncing like a leprechaun and screaming, "*Woo-hoo!*" as he went.

"Wigs, I get it. It's a rough night for you. Some strange guy is macking on your woman and no one is loving you. But I gotta tell you, you're not winning any favors. You gotta get your butt out of my face, buddy. It's really squelching my game."

I giggled. We were spooning in my bed. It had to be five a.m. We'd been up most of the night, talking and grinding and dry humping. It was a real straight-out-of-your-high-school-playbook kind of a night. Luke was torturing me. He hadn't made a single attempt to get into my jeans, and while I didn't want to go to bone town, I wanted his fingers circling my clit.

"What time is it?" he asked. "I think I have to go soon."

I pressed my tush back into his crotch. "So soon?" I whined.

"Hmm..." He dipped his head down, lavishing my neck with wet kisses. "Trust me, I'd stay if I could, but my brothers will be all over my ass if I keep them waiting on me."

He was hard, pressing against my backside. I rolled my hips against him and then said, "I kind of like you over my ass, right now."

He snickered. "That was a terrible segue."

I pretended to be offended. "Shut up. You loved it. You think I'm the funniest, sexiest woman you've ever met."

In complete seriousness, he said, "I do."

My heart leaped in my chest.

He made no move to leave. Instead, he started kissing my neck again. I moaned and pushed back into him, rutting my hips more and more desperately. He slipped his hand up, palming my breast. My nipple puckered instantly. It had been that way all night. My body responded to him as if he were issuing commands. Wherever he touched, compliance and pleasure followed. I wasn't alone now; he was breathing heavily in my ear and thrusting his hips in rhythm with mine.

"I was thinking," he said, his hand moving slowly down over my ribs, past my belly button, grazing the button of my jeans, "before I go..."

"Yes." I was way too eager. "Oh my God, yes." I even moved to unbutton my jeans for him. And then, finally, after what felt like an eternity of the most delicious torture ever, his fingers slipped under the elastic of my panties. I knew what it was like down there; it was a goddamn rain forest.

As he slipped his fingers into my seriously humid situation, he made a sound, a deep guttural sound—an animal in heat sound. "Jesus, Maddie, not today. But I want to be in here." He pushed his own force of nature against me as punctuation. "You're so wet."

I was so wet.

He bit my shoulder just right, and electricity shot through me.

I'm not quiet. Some women are quiet. If you ask me, no one is naturally like porn. But I'm one of the few that moan the whole way through, not scream. I pant and coo and cry out. And I was babbling, bursting, and breathing all kinds of little noises. I couldn't control it. Every circle of his fingers had me humming with pleasure.

He loved it. "Fuck, Maddie, these little sounds. You're gonna make me mess my pants."

His words brought me back to the feeling of his cock pressed against me. Everywhere, muscles tightened.

"That's it, baby…" he breathed against my ear. "Come for me."

And I did.

Let me just say, it was a double whopper, a toe-curling, heart-pounding, skin-flushing, teeth-numbing orgasm, with a big fat capital O.

When I came down from seeing stars, I flipped over so I was facing him and said, "Wigs is so never talking to you again."

"Doesn't take well to legit competition, huh?" He tucked a blue strand behind my ear.

We were so close, our faces inches apart.

"I had such a good time tonight," he said.

"Me too."

"Can I see you later?" he asked.

I nodded.

"After work?"

I nodded again.

He kissed me. First my lips, then my forehead. "I'll be counting the minutes." He stood and I went to get up too. "No." He leaned over to kiss me one more time. Then he said, "Get under the covers and get some rest. I'll see you later."

"Good." I smiled.

After he showed himself out, I lay in my bed, giddy and glowing. Wigs showed up, head-butting my hand, looking for love. I threaded my fingers through fur, waiting for the purr.

"Guess what, Mr. Wiggles?"

He didn't answer but he rammed his little skull against my fingers a second time.

"Mama's got a boyfriend."

9

LUKE

few weeks after my first date with Maddie, my sister, Sarah, called, bordering on annoyed.

"Luke, I don't mean to pry..." she said.

But she did really. That's exactly what she meant to do.

She continued. "I feel like you're living a double life. What is going on with you?" She was gentle but insistent.

"I'm not a spy, Sarah. Is no one in this family allowed to have a life outside the ranch?" I was a little too terse—terser than I should have been.

I startled her with my frustration and her voice was small when she said, "Of course you're allowed to have a life. I'd just like to be a part of it."

She reminded me so much of our mother. Sarah was wonderful, and it wasn't her fault that I felt unable to share myself with our family. In fact, she was the one I felt it would be easiest to talk to about my drawing and Maddie and everything else in my life.

"I'm sorry," I said. "You're right. What can I do to make it up to you?"

"Come to dinner on Sunday? I'll make vegetarian lasagna with tofu. It'll totally irritate Wyatt and Cody. Sound good?"

My sister was a spirited little thing; it was genetic. "Sounds perfect."

Honestly, I knew I had to make time to go back to the ranch and have supper or else my siblings were going to start showing up at my apartment and poking around the other parts of my life. They thrived on digging around in my life. Nothing better to do, I guess.

ON SUNDAY EVENING, the drive out to the ranch was lovely. Where we lived in Montana, you didn't question why they called it Big Sky Country. It was April and the weather had shifted from cold to mild. The rolling hills of grass were lush and green; the sky was dotted with cotton ball clouds, and it felt like you could see clear across the county to the mountains in the distance. I loved Montana. I loved my home and my siblings. I loved my day job, loved being on the land, caring for the animals. I also loved to draw, and I thought I might be fallin' in love with a certain blue-haired beauty. I was a lucky man. It was warm enough that I opened the window, resting my arm on the sill and letting my fingers push through the rushing air. I felt free and happy. All was good in my world. Thankfully, I carried this carefree feeling with me into my father's house because from the minute I walked through the door, I felt like I was at an intervention.

"Howdy," I hollered, shutting the door behind me.

Cody, who was bounding down the stairs that faced the door, said, "Can I help you? I think you might have the wrong house."

I rolled my eyes at him and headed for the kitchen. Wyatt was leaning against the counter; Bill was sitting in a chair next to the old corded phone that hung on the wall, and Sarah was pulling her lasagna out of the oven.

Wyatt continued Cody's ribbing by actually screaming like a girl. "Please, mister, take what you want. Just don't hurt us."

Sarah swatted him with her oven mitt. "Leave him alone, you big oaf. He's here now."

My father, who usually left the banter to my brothers, called from the living room, "Did I hear the bellow of my second oldest son? I thought he'd taken ill and was laid up and dying of cholera."

"No, Dad. It was dysentery," Bill called back.

"Such a shame," my father said, walking into the room. "I told him not to try to forge that river with his wagon, but what can I tell you? Second sons never listen. Hopefully, we can salvage his oxen and still go for gold."

"Are the two of you having fun?" I asked.

"Come on, bro. Oregon Trail humor is some highbrow stuff," Bill said.

"You do realize that I see y'all every day?" I chastised.

"Seeing you on a horse, working the ranch is not seeing you," my father argued. "We're a family. We expect you here to break bread on the regular, son."

Underneath his codgy exterior, my father was a real softy. I knew what he was saying was that he missed me, so I replied to that.

"I missed you too," I said. "I'm sorry. I've got a lot on my plate."

Cody, who was setting the table in the dining room, called out, "From what I heard, it's a blue-plate special."

"What's he talking about?" Sarah asked me and then looked at Wyatt to see if he knew.

Wyatt smirked. "A certain brand-new Conway resident has been seen around town with Luke."

"A girl?" Sarah asked.

"No, a Chihuahua," Wyatt replied.

My father grumbled, "That explains it," and then headed to the dining room.

Sarah looked back to me, giddy as could be. "You met a girl," she squealed. Then her face contorted. "Wait, why did Cody say blue-plate special? Is that some gross sexist comment that I'm gonna have to punch him for?"

"No," I said, offering nothing else.

Wyatt clarified, gossiping with Sarah like he was a coquette. "Her hair is blue."

"Oh," Sarah's eyes popped. "I've heard about her."

"Cute as a button," Wyatt winked. "And she's got sass too."

"I heard she's more than cute, Wyatt. Rosemarie got her hair cut last week and she came out of the salon talking about dying her hair blue. Can you imagine Rosemarie with blue hair?" Sarah rolled her eyes while putting her oven mitts back on to carry the lasagna into the dining room. "Anyway, what's her name, Luke?"

Reluctantly, I offered, "Madison."

Wyatt, Bill, and I followed Sarah into the dining room as she continued. "Madison is apparently so attractive that Rosemarie got it in her head that she might get some additional traction with the guys in town just by reminding them of her."

The hairs on the back of my neck stood up. I hated thinking of other men in town looking at Maddie.

"No one's dating her but me," I said.

Everyone at the table turned and looked at me.

Bill laughed. "A little heavy-handed there, brother. No one even mentioned her dating anyone else."

Wyatt banged his chest with his fists. "Me, Luke. She, Maddie. She mine."

My father, who again generally refrained from getting involved, laughed. I think he felt happy that I was dating. Bill was always going on about how Dad was a romantic, but I'd never seen it myself.

Sarah looked at Wyatt who was sitting next to her and whispered, "He likes her."

"I met her," Wyatt whispered back.

"You did?" Sarah gushed.

"We can all hear you both," Cody said incredulously.

"They know that, Cody," I said.

He shrugged. "Well then, why pretend to whisper? Whatever. I met her too." He eyed Sarah, knowing full well she'd be jealous. Being twins, they were always a bit competitive. It was bizarre because they were so different. Sarah was creative and driven. Cody was more like Wyatt—wild, haphazard, and not quite sure where he belonged.

Sarah turned her injustice on me. "They both met her and I didn't?"

I interjected. "I didn't introduce them. They got haircuts."

But Sarah kept talking right over me. "That is so unfair. I made you tofu lasagna."

Wyatt and Cody both groaned.

"Maybe I need a haircut too," Sarah said, still pouting.

Leaning over the middle of the table, my father cut himself a big square of tofu lasagna. It hit his plate with a splat. Then he settled back into his seat and said with an impish smile, "I'm getting my hair cut tomorrow."

Oh, for heaven's sake.

10

MADDIE

"How many weeks is it now?" Delores asked. She was constantly nosing around for information about my relationship with Luke. I wasn't sure if it was a living vicariously thing or a gossipy habit thing, but it was definitely a thing.

A woman named Wanda, whose hair I had cut twice, was in my chair. Wanda was the kind of woman that wore a lot of lipstick and had good intentions but might not always live up to them. She asked, "Are you two talking about Luke Morgan? That's who you're dating. Right, Maddie?"

This town. I had no doubt that Wanda was one hundred percent certain that Luke was my man. We had been dating for exactly one month today, and everyone in town seemed to know that we were together, but to me, they all pretended like they might have heard something about it.

I smiled. "Yes. I'm dating Luke." Then I grasped a chunk of her hair, lined it up with my comb, and prepared to cut.

"He sure is a looker," Wanda said. "All those Morgan boys are so handsome."

"That is the truth," Delores echoed.

"I bet he's more than looks," Wanda hinted, trying to imply that Luke was good in bed. "When I was a teenager, I happened to see Bill Morgan lose his trunks at the swimming hole. Wyatt played a prank on him. All I can say is that boy was packing some heat, if you know what I mean."

Delores laughed. She was resting in one of the hairdryer seats. She had a magazine on her lap and looked a little tired. It had been a long day. "That wasn't exactly subtle, Wanda. We all know what you mean."

I said nothing. Admittedly, I certainly had a stronger familiarity with Luke's assets than either of these women, but honestly, even though we started out all hot and heavy, we'd been taking it really slow. I mean, I've touched it, and for sure, my man was working with some serious equipment. But the day after our first date, we sat down and had a long discussion about the emotional versus the physical. Luke said he'd been out on the ranch thinking about me coming on his fingers and he was struck by the reality that he wanted to savor each phase of our sexual exploration. It sounded insane to me. What guy wants to wait for any reason other than maybe the belief in no sex before marriage? But the more he talked about it, the more I got what he was trying to say to me.

He said, "Obviously, neither one of us are virgins, right?"

I smirked but nodded. We were sitting in my kitchen eating Chinese food out of the cartons.

"Okay, well, do you agree that there was something magical about the sexual experiences you had before you had sex? All the hot and heavy making out?"

"Of course, but sex is good too."

"No doubt," he said, implying my point was obvious with his tone.

"But, ugh. How do I explain this?" He paused, his eyes rolling up as he tried to put his thoughts together. "I don't just want to get into a routine where we take off our clothes and flop into bed, hump, and go to sleep. I want to learn how to make each other crazy. I want to know everything there is to know about your body before I slip inside you, Maddie. It's like there is this other plane of sex, not just crazy lust-fueled fucking, which honestly, a part of me is dying to jump into, but I want more than that with you. I want to be the best you've ever had, and I'm a realist so that's gonna take work and knowledge. I want us to learn each other's rhythms before we bang. This is insane. I'm being insane, right?"

It was actually totally hot. "Not insane exactly. What are we talking about here? A week? A month? A year? Or just by ear?"

"How about until we can't stand it anymore?"

"So, by ear then," I quipped.

He laughed. And that was pretty much the deal since then.

A part of me wanted to spill all of this to Wanda and Delores. I wanted to tell them that he was a genius. That his idea to wait and play sexual explorers had my heart racing with desire all day. If he sent me a text message that said,

"Hi," I was instantly wet. Every touch was burned into my memory and I thought about being sexy with him all day long. But I kept my thoughts to myself. I didn't need everyone in town knowing that Luke Morgan was by far the sexiest man I'd even been with and I hadn't even been with him yet.

"Not gonna give us even a tiny taste, are you, Maddie?" Delores asked.

"Nope." I set up another section of Wanda's hair. "But I will tell you we have a date tonight."

"Talk is," Wanda offered. "That you two are pretty serious." She, like all my other clients, was just prodding me, seeing if she could be the one to crack the surface and get the details they all wanted to throw around at their book clubs, sewing circles, and church luncheons.

I smiled at her, making it look like I was just holding my cards close to my chest, but she was right. It felt serious. Except, I knew what Luke didn't know... that I couldn't have babies. I had to talk to him about it. I had started waking up at night, when he was there and when he wasn't, terrified that once he knew I was barren, it would all be over. A part of me knew that it should be. A man as good as Luke deserved to raise children. The world needed children raised by people like Luke. Men and women with love to give. People nothing like my parents.

"Cathy Higgins. You know her, don't you, Maddie? She told me last week that she has never seen Luke so twisted up in knots about a woman and she's known him since preschool."

Wanda had also known Luke since preschool. Considering she'd pretended that she wasn't certain who I was dating five minutes earlier, I wasn't too surprised that she'd been discussing my relationship with Cathy Higgins.

I shrugged my shoulders. "I wouldn't know."

"Leave her alone, Wanda. Just because your life is uninspired at the moment doesn't mean you can get her to tell you her secrets." Delores was protecting me; she usually jumped in about this time in a conversation about Luke and me.

"Aww, pshaw, you're only saying that because you probably know more details than the rest of us."

"Nope." Delores opened the magazine on her lap. "She keeps her daydreams close and her reality closer. It's what I like most about her."

So, yes, Delores was nosy, but she was also the best.

AFTER WORK I RAN HOME, showered, and got dressed for a BBQ. Luke and I were going to Anthony's house; his family was having a get-together. It was the first time I was going to be out and about with people from the art class, other than Luke. I still hadn't gone completely bare and I talked to Anthony a few times with Luke, but I knew others from the class could be there and I had to admit, I felt a little exposed. That said, this was my goal, right? To get comfortable with my body through trial by fire, so best to just take a deep breath and run over the coals, amiright?

Luke picked me up around five thirty, but since Anthony lived in Fletcher, we didn't get there until after six. Anthony lived in a smaller home, when you considered how many people were living in it. Anthony was one of two in his generation still living in his parents' house. His oldest sister also lived there with her children. She was recently divorced with two kids, something that apparently troubled her Catholic grandma, who also lived in the house. Anthony's parents made jokes about moving out and leaving them all behind. It was a real family gathering, warm and filled with rousing banter. Something utterly unfamiliar to me. Luke seemed to fit right in. There were attendees of all ages— grandmas to newborns. I settled into chatting with Anthony's other sister, Carmela, not the divorced one. She was rocking her newborn in her arms. Our conversation, as usual, began as a comment about my hair, and then, as usual, once she realized I was a stylist, shifted to a conversation about her hair. I was trying to be in the moment and pay attention to her, but just over her shoulder, Luke was playing with Anthony's other sister's kids.

Someone had set up a game of cornhole. Luke and the kids weren't the slightest bit concerned with the rules of the game. Instead, they were just throwing the bean bags and cheering or laughing, depending on where the bag landed. Luke seemed perfectly content to spend his time with them, encouraging them, advising them about how to throw better, roaring with celebration when they got the bean bag in the hole. As I peeked over Carmela's shoulder, my first instinct was just to smile. It must have been a glowy, gooey smile because Carmela turned to see what had caught my attention.

"You're lucky. It looks like he'd make a great dad," she said. "Lord knows, they don't all inherit that gene."

At her words, the world crumbled beneath my feet. Watching him with those kids, it was crystal clear. Luke was meant to be a dad. He was so good with kids, an absolute natural. Suddenly, I could imagine him with his own children, perfection. I could see them in my mind, little towheaded boys that grew up to have dark beards, a daughter named Molly after his mother, car seats in his truck, and tiny cowboy boots. There was no room for my broken blue-haired body in that picture because I couldn't give him those things. Luke could never truly be mine. I had to end it. I had to tell him the whole truth. Tonight. Let the chips fall where they may. In the end, it would be better that we never made love. Best to not have to remember that for the rest of my life.

THE REST of the evening was garbage. I tried to be pleasant and enjoy myself, but I couldn't seem to get beyond my own anxiety about blowing up my relationship with Luke, so I basically acted withdrawn and a little bitchy. When we pulled up in front of my house after a long drive of one-word answers and intermittent silence, Luke said, "Maddie, what is up with you? Are you okay?"

"Yeah, um, just sad I guess." I popped open the truck door and headed for the house. Usually, he helped me get out, an excuse for us to get close. But I didn't want to lose my nerve, so it was probably best if he didn't touch me. He'd been spending almost every night at my place, so I wasn't surprised he followed me.

"Is it something I did?" he asked, catching up from behind me.

"No, God, no. I just..." I didn't want to do this on the front lawn. "Come on," I said, pointing casually toward the front door. "Let's talk inside."

It took me a second to get my key out of my purse. He sidled up behind me, pressing his lips into my hair, the smell of him enveloping me like a fog. I tensed at his touch, the sadness of what I had to do screaming in my chest.

As always, he was exceptionally sensitive to my feelings. "You are mad," he said, stepping back.

I found the keys and opened the door. "I'm not. I have to talk to you about something."

"Are you breaking up with me?" he asked.

"No, but I have to tell you something and it's hard." I dropped my purse on the kitchen table. My kitchen and living room were a pretty open floor plan. I crossed to my forest-green couch and sat down. It was a good deep couch. The kind a person curls up in. I let it engulf me. He followed me into the living room and stood there, the coffee table between us. He looked nervous.

"Are you from another planet and you have to go back?" he asked, trying to lighten the mood.

I laughed, and then I started crying. He was just too good. Too perfect. I didn't want to lose him. I didn't want to be with someone else. I didn't want him to be with someone else. I never really knew if I wanted kids, but with Luke, I would want kids. And suddenly, I felt crushed that I was losing the children that I could never have. I sobbed, and instinctively, he ran to me, wrapped me up in his arms, and held me hard to his chest so that I could feel the rhythm of his heartbeat against my cheek.

"Fuck, baby. What can I do?" he asked, peppering the crown of my head with kisses.

I needed him. I wanted him. Why did this happen to me? Why wasn't I allowed to have a future with this man?

As if he could hear my fears, he said, "Whatever it is. It will be okay. We can make it okay." Even though he didn't really know what he was agreeing to, I allowed myself to take a breath.

"Can you kiss me?" I asked.

He smiled. "Always." And then his lips were on mine. He kissed me hard, trying to drive the sadness from my mind. I let him. I let him coax me with his passion, let his touch make me forget why it was so important to tell him the secret I was keeping.

I would have to tell him, eventually. Just not tonight.

Maddie was sitting across from me at the diner we liked to stop at after class. It was a classic 50s style diner that resembled the old train car, complete with a neon red diner sign, chrome roof, and windows all across the front. It reminded me of *Nighthawks* and sometimes sitting there, I pictured us, her blue hair and my cowboy hat painted into Edward Hopper's masterpiece. Honestly, the food wasn't great, but it was on the road from Fletcher to Conway and it had kinda become our place. We both ordered grilled cheese and French fries. I was about finished with mine, but Maddie hadn't taken more than a bite or two. She was absolutely over the moon. Tonight, she faced our class without a stitch of fabric covering her skin, and she was literally glowing with excitement.

"It was so much better than I suspected it would be," she gushed. "I didn't feel shame at all. I didn't feel like anyone was staring or judging. I just felt free, ya know? Like I deserved to be looked at and appreciated."

She did, by me. Besides that one instance where Maddie freaked out after Anthony's family's BBQ, everything with us had fallen into place. For me, it was a pretty insane experience. We'd been dating for a couple of months now and I only wanted her more each day. For the record, I wanted her, not just sex with her. I wanted to be with her every second of the day. My brothers were constantly teasing me for texting her and calling her and running off to be with her. She was funny and smart and just so cool. She was my favorite friend I ever had. Don't get me wrong, I wanted sex with her too, badly. We were still maintaining our slow-moving sexual exploration policy, and I was finding it harder to control my urge to pin her up against the wall and ravish her body in the way we both craved. But my idea to move slowly had turned out to be a stroke of genius. I thought I was going to last a few days, but instead, we'd lasted weeks, and with each day, our desire for each other increased. We were like rabbits, only without the screwing.

We couldn't keep our hands off each other. Maddie was coming on my fingers multiple times a day. But she was also coming from the sound of my voice. Sometimes she called me from work, locked in the bathroom, turned on because she was thinking of me. She'd tell me things like she got to thinking about my tongue circling her nipples, slowly and interminably, like I had not a care in the world, and how the thought of it got stuck in her head until she was wet and writhing. She'd say something like, "I wish you were here."

The first time she called me like this, all hot and bothered, I instructed her to go into the bathroom. She was quiet.

"Do it, go to the bathroom, Maddie," I said.

I heard the shuffle of her movement through the phone and the closing of the door. Then, even though no one could hear her, she whispered, "Now what?" She sounded nervous and a little bit scared, but also willing.

"I want you to close your eyes," I paused. I could hear her breathe. "Are they closed?"

"Yes," she said quietly.

"I want you to imagine that I am standing right behind you, so close that you can feel the warmth of my body on your back. Can you feel me?" I kept my voice husky and deep.

"Yes."

"Your bare shoulder is responding to the heat of my breath as I slowly inch closer to you. How does it feel?" In my head, she was leaning on the sink counter in front of the mirror with her eyes closed, listening to my voice.

"Good, so good," she whispered breathily.

"My lips are closing in on the nape of your neck. As they land on your sweet skin, I bite down gently. Do you like that?"

"Uh-huh," she whimpered.

"As I am kissing and nibbling on every part of your neck and shoulders, I wrap my hands around your luscious ass. How does it feel?"

"I love to feel you on me," she panted.

"Are you ready for me? Can you feel my hands parting your thighs?" I questioned.

"You have no idea," she said with a ring of truth to it.

"I need you to do something for me, Maddie. I need you to make two of your fingers my tongue. I need my tongue between your thighs. Can you feel my tongue, warm and wet on your sweet little pussy, Maddie?"

"Yes," she said in a lustful cry.

"How does it feel?"

"Incredible. Oh, Luke," she cried out.

"My tongue is circling your clit right now, but it longs to be deeper."

She moaned. I could picture her bucking against her own fingers in the bathroom at the salon.

"I am pushing my fingers inside you now. Thick and hard, deep inside you." Picturing my cock inside her turned me on too. "Damn, baby." I groaned. "You're so wet. I'm dying to fuck you. Can I, Maddie?"

"Yes. Fuck, yes," she exclaimed.

"I am deep inside you, Maddie." She was losing it now, her breath and sounds quickening. Maddie was not a quiet lover, but I knew that if she made too much noise, Delores would hear her. "I love those noises you're making, but I'm covering your mouth. We have to be quiet, baby. We don't want to get caught fucking in the bathroom."

The phone clattered and I literally heard her squelch her noises with her hand as she came hard. When all was silent, she picked up the phone again.

"Was it good for you?" she asked, making me laugh.

I had no doubt that when we really did fuck, it was going to be intense.

In the present moment, at the table in the diner, Maddie continued to expound on her evening's success. I loved how high and happy her success made her and I was so proud of her that she achieved what she set out to do, but I'm not gonna lie, for the first hour, having her bare in front of me was rough. First of all, it wasn't my favorite thing to have all those eyes on her. I had to control myself from snatching pencils out of my fellow classmates' hands and scolding them until they turned away. I'd never been so possessive in my life. But this was about her journey, so being some whacked-out tyrant was not an option.

Secondly, much like Maddie, I was turned on by her at the drop of a hat. So, while tonight wasn't the first time I had seen her naked, it was different. In class, I was granted license to just look, to just devour her with my eyes, and it was more than my poor dick could handle. I literally had to tuck my erection into the waist of my pants, like I did when I was thirteen, so I didn't throw a full-on tent in class. During the break, she threw on her robe and some flip-flops and headed out to the bathroom to pee. I waited by the door of the ladies' room and when she came out, I pulled her into a nearby dark classroom. It was a lab-style room with tall counters all around.

I couldn't help myself. I pressed her against the wall right next to the door and drove my tongue into her mouth like a fucking tank. I was on the verge of exploding as soon as I touched her elbow in the hall. She pushed me back against one of the counter height desks. She was feeling powerful and I liked it.

As she unbuckled my belt and unbuttoned my jeans, she said, "Is this what you need? My hand on your cock?" And then it was. Her feminine fingers circled the head and pushed down.

All I said was, "Fuuuuck."

She kept talking. "You like watching me up there? Knowing that I belong to you? That I tremble at the thought of you?"

"Yes."

She was stroking me while she breathed her words against my ear. "You know what I've been thinking about lately?" she asked, but she didn't pause for me to answer. "I've been thinking about how much I want to taste you. To drop to my knees and feel the silk of your cock on my tongue."

That was it. That was all it took, the image of her before me, that blue hair a river down her back, the round of her ass pressing into the heels of her feet, her eyes looking up, her mouth open and willing, wanting even. I blew my load all over her hand.

She teased me for coming so quickly. "Pent-up, lately?"

"I think you have some idea," I teased back. She kissed my neck just below my ear and then crossed to the sink at the front of the classroom to wash her sticky hands.

I spoke across the room. "Honestly," I whined. "It was a feat that I didn't come the instant you touched me. I'm going crazy in there."

She crossed back to me. She softly kissed my lips and then said, "I'm not gonna lie, I love that." She shivered, then she bit her bottom lip. "Hmm... the thought of you all hard-up and hungry for me. Delicious."

I laughed, grabbed her hips, and pulled her against me. "Good," I rumbled.

She kissed me again, wet and growly this time. Then she broke away. "We need to get back. Me first," she said, walking backwards to the door.

I groaned, clawing at the empty space she left behind and pushing out my bottom lip in a pout.

Before she left the room, she said, "Don't you worry, cowboy. We can play more later." Then she winked and she was gone. I stood there for a minute or two before following her back to class to endure another hour of her brand of titillating torture that seemed specifically designed for me, only, the second hour was different than the first.

Once my overzealous little friend reached his happy ending, I was able to focus on drawing her. My hands seemed to have a mind of their own. And I'm not going to lie, I think my familiarity with Maddie had something to do with it. It felt like all our sexual exploration was actually part of my work as an artist, like she was always a work of art to me. All my passion for her sexually was also a passion for her artistically. Every touch, every line, every kiss, every shadow... they were all related. The artist in me knew her, felt her in each stroke, and that knowledge of her beauty, her sweetness, poured out of me onto the page. Needless to say, drawing a naked Maddie was something I definitely wanted to do more, perhaps in private.

Finally preparing to eat more of her grilled cheese, Maddie looked across the table at me and asked, "So, I'm fairly certain I have a good grasp of what you were thinking during the first hour of class, but you seemed to have a different experience in the second hour. What was it like for you, having me up there..." She peeked around to see if anyone was eavesdropping and then lowered her voice to a whisper when she said, "Naked?"

"I liked it," I said, smiling mischievously because I knew that wasn't going to be close to enough for her inquiring mind. She wanted to know me as deeply as I was looking to know her.

She had picked up her drink to take a sip, and in response to my answer, she slammed it down on the table and the root beer inside the glass sloshed around. "Oh, come on, Luke. Give me more than that. You were so different in the second hour. In the first hour, you were like a drooling fool—"

I interrupted her. "You mean, I was like an Adonis in the prime of his manhood."

"Yeah, that's it, a sex-crazed gerbil." She smirked. She was so fucking beautiful. She was in a maroon hoodie with her hair tied in a messy blue knot on the top of her head.

"Good to know we agree on this point," I said with a straight face and she snickered.

"Anyway, you were hot to trot in the beginning, but then you were so focused. I don't think I've ever seen you draw like that."

"Yeah, you should definitely give me handy before class all the time," I teased. "Does wonders for my concentration."

She threw her napkin at me. "Come on, I'm being serious."

"Sorry." I smiled. "You're right. You've never seen me draw like that. I've never seen me draw like that. At least, not that I remember."

She bounced in her seat, giddy with excitement. "Can I see them?" she asked. "Your drawings?"

I wasn't one of those people who never showed anyone my art. Like I told Maddie on our first date, I'd always drawn pictures anywhere and everywhere, but since starting this class, I kept my sketches to myself. It was my first real art class and I didn't want to invite any criticism just yet. I was literally awake at night worrying about the student exhibition that was the culmination of our class because I didn't know if I was good enough. Honestly, I didn't think Maddie would judge me, but I'd also never drawn someone the way I was drawing Maddie. I wasn't ready yet.

I stumbled, trying to answer her. "I... um... Maddie, I..."

She threw her hands up defensively, "Don't worry. It's fine."

But it wasn't. She was disappointed; I could see it in her eyes.

She continued. "You don't have to show me. I get it. It's personal."

I wanted her to actually get it, but I wasn't sure how to explain. "It's not that exactly. I'm just not ready. I promise to show them to you first; you can even help me pick which ones are in the class exhibition. It's just right now they aren't finished and I don't trust myself as an artist, and it's like this part of me that feels vulnerable. I don't know that I can capture you, that I can do you justice. You're just so beautiful, Maddie. You're this giant vibrant life and I'm just a rancher pretending to be an artist."

"Okay," she said, seemingly happy again. "But I bet they are good, your sketches."

"You just like me." I smiled.

"Well, yes, but also all the other students were looking at what you were working on."

That was a surprise. "They were?"

She nodded.

"Are you sure that wasn't during the first half of class, the part where my raging hard-on was bursting out of my pants like it was reenacting that scene from *Aliens*?"

She laughed. God, I loved making her laugh.

"I'm sure," she reiterated.

"Maddie?" I asked. "I was thinking. I'd like to draw you more."

"What do you mean?" She looked at me quizzically.

Suddenly, I was nervous. I wanted her to let me draw her whenever I wanted. "I mean, I was wondering if you'd let me bring an easel to the house and if you'd maybe pose for me?"

"Do you want to draw me like one of your French girls, Jack?"

"*Titanic*, really?"

"Come on, it's a spot-on reference. And also, clearly more current than *Aliens*."

"He dies in the end."

"Maybe I'm a praying mantis."

I laughed. "I think it'd still be worth it."

She took a bite of her grilled cheese.

"So, will you? Pose for me?" I asked again, needing verbal confirmation.

She looked at me, looked hard. And then she said, "I think I will."

12

MADDIE

L uke carried his art supplies inside in two trips. He was quiet and acting a little jittery. Once everything was inside, he asked, "Where should I set up?"

"That's up to you. Where do you want me?" I winked.

"Umm..." He pulled off his cowboy hat and scratched his head. "I should have thought about it. I didn't think about it. Maybe we can move the coffee table and you can lie on the couch?"

Not buying it. He thought about it maybe a little too much. "Sure, the couch is fine."

"I think the contrast would be good. The green against your skin."

Definitely thought about it. "Okay." I smiled. "Whatever works. Do you need anything?" I asked. "A glass of water?"

"I'm good. Also, I kinda know where everything is, Maddie," he smiled.

"Right." I shifted in place. It occurred to me that I was being a little odd too.

"I guess I should..." I pointed to the couch, not sure what to do with myself.

"If you want." He smiled. "I'll just be right here, getting set up."

"Yeah, okay." I started to walk in the direction of the couch. He stepped toward me, then pulled me in and hugged me, burying his face in my hair.

"I'm nervous," he said quietly. "I need to kiss you. I didn't kiss you when I got here, did I?"

He hadn't. I shook my head. He tipped my chin up with his hand and gently fluttered his lips against mine. It was a sweet kiss. The kind of kiss that says you mean something to me. The kind of kiss that is begging for meaning in return. I kissed him back just as gently and with just as much meaning. I was falling, fast. With our foreheads pressed together and our eyes closed, we both took a deep breath.

When we broke apart, I headed for the couch again. This time, he smacked my ass. I giggled and posed like Betty Boop, with my ankle lifted and my hand over my mouth in a feigned gesture of innocent surprise. It was a little moment, but one that was more normal for us than the weird nervousness he walked in with.

I sat on the couch with my hands tucked under my knees. Watching him situate his easel, I felt strangely shy. Lying naked before him on my couch felt a long way away from sitting posed before the classroom. There was a certain clinical nature to modeling for a room full of art students. As the model, you were bathed in the classroom's collective consciousness, their unified belief that you were a thing of beauty, elevated above sexuality. But being naked alone with Luke was different. On an average day, I was dying to be naked around this man. For the record, there were literally multiple instances where I had pulled off my clothes before we could get the door to the house closed. But there was something about this moment, something more exposed. When we were being sexy together, our focus was sexy time. When I was modeling in the class, the focus was the art form. But tonight, when I stretched out on my own couch, I felt like the focus would be on me.

Not wanting to lose my nerve, I shifted from my own discomfort to watching him. Luke was meticulous. He had his easel set up and he was pulling my kitchen table next to it so that he could surround himself with his supplies. He had pencils, charcoal, and pastels. He also had erasers and those white pointy things that artists use to blend stuff. He laid them all out neatly on the table.

He was wearing jeans and a gray t-shirt. He had recently hung his hat by the door. A couple of weeks ago, I put a hook there, so he had a place for his hat that Mr. Wiggles couldn't access. Prior to the hook, Wigs had taken to cuddling with Luke's hat and leaving a furry gray trail in his wake. There is a certain sex appeal to a man in a hat, but I liked Luke without his. His hair was thick and straight, highlighted naturally by the sun. It was the kind of blond hair that women dream about and spend their whole lives trying to attain, only when it was framing this rugged masculine face, it lost all its femininity and became something wholly male. Like usual, he had it pulled back into a quick loose bun at the nape of his neck. This man was such a magical collision of things. A cowboy who couldn't eat cows. A rugged man with so many soft edges. A brother who was keeping his creative heart from his family but couldn't seem to be anything but honest in his daily interactions. He felt so authentic to me—so raw and true.

I watched him until he checked and double-checked his materials. Once he was certain they were as he wished, he crossed to a kitchen chair, sat down, and took off his boots and socks.

"Whenever I'm in class, I wish I was barefoot." The way he said the words made them feel like a secret. "I always draw barefoot at home."

He actually had really sexy feet. Like the rest of him, they looked strong, like they were rooting him to the earth.

I smiled at the private detail, "Mi casa es su casa," I offered.

He stood. "Well, I guess I'm all set."

I tried to sound jovial and free-spirited when I said, "Okay, boss, how do you want me?" But it came out clunky and uncomfortable.

Maybe trying to quiet my nerves, he said, "Why don't we just start by taking off your top, leave everything else on and lean back a little and we can slowly progress to a more," he paused, searching for the right word, "classic pose," aka naked, or as artists like to say, nude.

I crossed my arms in front of me and pulled my t-shirt over my head, tossing it next to me on the couch. Being shirtless before him didn't feel shocking or soul-bearing. It felt normal, but the thought of removing the other items of clothing still had me rattled. I leaned back a little, pushing my breasts out and lifting my heart. I used my hands to balance, shaking my hair out so that it fell away from my shoulders.

"Like this?" I asked, confirming I was as he wanted me.

He bit his lower lip. "Yes... turn your chin slightly to the right. Good, I want to study your face. I am always at an angle in class. Are you comfortable?" he asked.

I adjusted a touch. It was a thing I had learned to do after my first few times modeling, check in with my body to make sure I could comfortably hold my position for a while. I decided I could, and then I slowed my breaths and stilled.

He took a charcoal pencil and put it to the paper, but then he put it down again.

"The light isn't right," he muttered, crossing the room to adjust the curtains and then moving a novelty lamp that was sitting on one on the couch's side tables. The lamp was akin to the lamp in *A Christmas Story*, a giant fish-netted gamb, wearing a red heel and topped off with a lampshade. What can I say? I liked kitsch. Luke pulled the shade off the leg, exposing the raw light bulb. I imagined that with a brighter light off to my right, he'd created more shadows, but to be honest, I didn't know much about lighting. He returned to his position behind his easel and looked at me again.

"That's better." He said the words to himself, and then he immediately began to sketch. He worked feverishly, using multiple pencils, holding them in his teeth and tucking them behind his ears. From my seated position, I was looking up at him. He'd glance at me. Sometimes his eyes would meet mine, other times, he'd just briefly focus on whatever aspect he was working on, and then his eyes would return to the drawing before him. In general, he was quiet, an occasional instruction here or there, but overall focused on his work.

It was warm in the room. It rarely got really hot in Montana, but today was unseasonably warm and with all the lights, there was a sheen of sweat on his skin and mine.

After a bit, he slowed. He removed the sketch he'd been working on from the easel, placing it down on the table. I couldn't see it. I didn't try. I respected his need to show me on his own schedule.

"A break?" I questioned.

"Anytime you want," he replied.

I stood and stretched for a minute.

"You look beautiful," he said. He told me often. I gave him a little half-smile. Then I went to pee. When I came back, he had removed his t-shirt and was situating the pillows. Luke shirtless is a gift from all the gods. If Jesus, Buddha, Allah, Yahweh, and Vishnu ever had a powwow, it was to create Luke's torso. Broad shoulders, tight pecs, washboard abs, he was like sculpted marble.

"Is it naked time now?" I tried to tease but it came out quiet and introspective.

He nodded curtly, like he was trying not to make a big deal out of the whole thing.

I slipped my jeans off first, dropping them next to my discarded t-shirt. He was still standing close, waiting for me to lie on the couch so he could position me. I heard his deep intake of breath. He reached for me, running his hand over the cup of my bra, gently kneading my breast beneath the fabric. My nipples puckered instantly. I dropped my head back and a little guttural sound escaped. As if my noise alerted him to his own behavior, he dropped his hand back to his side, huffed air out his nose, and swallowed. I took a deep breath and unsnapped my bra and let it fall to the floor. Then I pulled down my panties and stood again.

My blue hair cascaded over my shoulders, covering my breasts. I thought of Botticelli's *Birth of Venus*. He took a step back, taking me in. He didn't know it, but he was giving me something. Something bigger than modeling in front of a class of strangers. Luke made me his muse and there was this giant bravery required to embody that role and it felt sexy and brazen and bold. My body was his to peruse—it was his to pose, his to have and devour. But it was mine. I was accepting my body as a thing worthy of his worship and granting him access.

"Lie down," he commanded, his voice rough with desire.

I did, but my heart was anything but relaxed. It raced in my chest like I was preparing to parachute out of an open plane door.

"Shift to your side, just a bit. Yes, like that." He crossed to me again, gently placing another pillow behind me. "Do you know Manet's *Olympia*?" he asked.

I nodded.

"I was thinking you could position yourself like that."

Shamelessly breathless, I said, "Show me what you want."

Again, he curtly nodded, maintaining some semblance of professionalism, but he was standing and I was lying on the couch, so from my vantage, I was well aware of how my nakedness was affecting him. He bent over me, running his hands up my sides until he got to my shoulders. He shifted the left one forward and the right one back. Then he propped my right elbow up on the pillow in such a way as to push forward my breastbone just a bit and reveal the fullness of my bust. Unlike Manet's *Olympia*, he draped my blue tresses so that they framed my breasts. As he worked, I became more and more aware that his breathing was as labored as mine.

He stepped back and then said, "Cross your ankles, left one on top."

I did.

"Now, bring that left hand forward and rest it on the top of your right thigh. Perfect." Almost giddy, he crossed back to the easel.

When I was modeling in class, I kept my mind on my goal, to feel at peace in my body, but this was different. I wasn't thinking about my relationship with my body at all. Instead, I was swimming in his reverence for my body. Luke's eyes swept over me, again and again. Each stroke of his pencil was a caress, rivers of charged energy plowing through me. Sometimes his glance lifted me up, elevating me in his awe, a kind of piety, a worshiping of me and other times, his eyes were overtaken by an almost irrational fervor, a craving, a kind of lecherous carnality that awoke a quiet storm of desire from deep in my core. With every inhalation, I felt the soft velvety fabric of the couch brushing against my back and thighs. My skin flushed, inflamed and hypersensitive. I desperately wanted to run my own hands over the softness of my body to try to calm and quench the feelings. But I stayed still, panting my breaths, trying not to beg him to put down his pencils and touch me.

"Can we talk?" I asked. "Or will it be distracting?"

"We can talk," he offered, but his mind was clearly still on his work. There was a long pause before he said, "Tell me what you're thinking."

"I'm thinking about you," I said simply because it was true.

His eyes jumped from the page to my face. He took me in from head to toe, and as his eyes moved over me, my skin pinked up even more. He could see it, the flush of my skin, the tension in my muscles, how wet and wanton I was for him.

"Tell me," he said, taking a bright-blue pastel from the table.

13

LUKE

"I'm thinking about touching you, the way your skin feels under my fingertips," Maddie answered and shifted a little bit, just her hips.

My grip on the pastel in my hand tightened. The drawing in front of me was the most beautiful work I had ever done, but I was so hard that I was literally aching. In all honesty, I'd been hard on the drive over. It was something about being trusted. But it was also this dirty bird in me that couldn't help but play out the fantasy, an artist and his muse. And the experience didn't disappoint, watching her, so confident, enchanting and open to me. I liked her this way, hungry and desperate for me. I burned hot, a little rabid. I had never really been into kinky stuff, but in the moment, I was enjoying the control. Maybe I was more that way than I realized. When I thought about it, all the deferral of sex we'd been experimenting with was also a certain kind of kink.

I dragged the pastel against the paper and she shivered.

"What else?" I asked, my voice demanding, dripping with my own desires.

"The salty taste of your sweat, the musky scent of you. It's almost unbearable how much I crave you," she cooed for me.

Her eyes closed, retreating to the visions in her head and she shifted again, more this time, bucking her hips off the couch just a bit.

Instinctually, I scolded her. "Now, now, no moving."

She opened her eyes and bit her lip. "But I want to move."

I wasn't going to last much longer. "Soon," I said, stroking the pastel to the paper again.

She was quiet for a few moments, looking right at me, and then she said, "I can't wait any longer."

There was nothing like this impertinent sexy woman. I smiled. "I promise. Just a few more seconds."

She didn't say anything right away, so I looked up from my work and once she knew she had my attention, she said, "That's not what I meant. I want you to fuck me."

I dropped the pastel and headed toward her. "Thank God."

She giggled as I dove for her, crawling hand over hand, kissing as I went until my fingertips were each resting on a thigh. Without a second thought, I lowered my face down and enveloped her clit in my mouth. I sucked. Pressing my tongue into her lush folds, I inadvertently growled my satisfaction. Maddie responded by digging her nails into the meat of my shoulders. Muffled, I asked, "Good?"

"Jesus Christ!" she roared with more force than I expected.

"Just me," I teased and then let out a slow-rolling hum, the sound reverberating against her juicy mound. She jumped a little and gasped, pushing her hips against my face.

"I can't wait," she whined. "I need you inside me."

Not one to deny my woman what she wants, I leaped up to strip off my pants. Maddie literally motioned her hands at me, like come back, come back. Our first time was supposed to be this long drawn-out fest, an all-night affair with candles and rose petals. I was supposed to make her come at least once before I entered her, but there was no stopping us now. And this moment was something better. We were hungry and happy and in love.

I was in love with Maddie.

I didn't think about it anymore than that. There was no hesitation. I pulled her to the edge of the couch, split her legs, and sunk my cock as far as I could into her pussy. I stayed upright on my knees and pushed in hard and desperate, rooted to her pelvis. I couldn't stop myself. I didn't pull out. Instead, I rolled my hips, teasing her sensitive nub. I wanted to stay buried so deep inside her that I couldn't tell where she ended and I began.

She cried out, "Luke... Luke."

My name on her lips made me buck. Maddie writhed and ground her hips against me, desperate for her release. I wanted more than just that. I lifted my hand and caressed her face. Her eyes found mine and locked on. I'd never looked someone in the eye while fucking before. She held me with her gaze, searing her spirit to mine. She was incredible like this, all animal, hungry, needy, passionate, sharing everything with me, baring her soul. The frenetic chaos of our lovemaking disappeared, replaced by a calm unified pulse, like our hearts were in sync. I'm sure there are better moments to tell someone how you feel, but I wanted her to know, I needed her to know right then, so I told her, "I love you."

She swallowed the words, ingested them like she was consuming an absolute delicacy, unbridled delight. First, the corners of her eyes lifted, then the corners of her mouth, and then her hands were on my chest and we were careening to the floor. As I hit the ground, I felt my cock pop out of her warmth and immediately felt the ache of wanting to return home. We were only separated for seconds before she climbed on top of me, fitting us back together. Little streams of happy tears flowed over her cheeks. When I reached to wipe them away with my thumb, I only succeeded in rubbing blue pastel on her skin.

"So much," she blurted, overwhelmed and giddy. "I love you so much." As soon as she'd said the words, she crashed forward, hugging her body to mine. When people talk about love, they reference their hearts, but my love for Maddie originated from a part of me that was more than muscle and blood. She was in every cell. I couldn't imagine breathing without her. Hearing her reciprocate my love, that was fucking priceless.

With my emotions soaring, I wrapped my arms around her while she kissed her way from my collarbone to my mouth. When she reached my lips, her kisses were deep and sultry, touching tongues, nipping teeth. Her hips gently pulsed, reinvigorating the heat we'd traded for emotion.

She rose up, rocking back and forth, riding me with a focused intensity. She palmed her own breasts, her blue hair everywhere, her head slightly thrown back, her lips parted, releasing the sounds of her rising pleasure. Fuck, if that wasn't the most glorious thing I'd ever seen. I couldn't help myself, I prayed. *Dear God, if by some chance I'm gonna die young, let this be the last thing I see.*

14

MADDIE

The bulk of my consciousness was lost to me, only able to captain the rising tide of pleasure coursing through my body. First, my muscles from cunt to crown clenched, and then the sensation began like a starburst, a ball of fire, radiating from my core, then a series of tiny spinning explosions. Everything unleashed at once, and my body was not mine. It was something ethereal, something floating among the stars.

Beneath me, Luke pounded his hips up and the pleasure coursed through me again, another fire, another explosion. It was like I couldn't stop coming. I heard his sounds, deep and guttural, growling and groaning. I could feel him swelling inside me.

"I'm too close," he called out. He tried to lift my hips to withdraw so that he didn't spill his seed. I wasn't going anywhere. I wanted all of him.

"Don't," I moaned. "I want you to come inside me."

"Yeah?" he questioned, his eyes bright with excitement, his voice shaking with the need to release.

I nodded and he didn't hesitate. He pulled my hips tight to his, thrust twice, and exploded. I felt it, the growing surge of his release, the pulse of his cock inside me, and then as if commanded by him, my starburst upgraded to the whole fucking sun and I was blind to everything but euphoria.

Shaking, I collapsed on his chest. I could hear his heart pounding and feel his sweat on my cheek. We were both out of breath, our panting heavy and hot. His hands found their way into my hair and he cradled my head to him.

With a loud sentiment but a quiet sound, he said, "I fucking love you."

"Me too," I said, barely coherent.

As if my love invigorated him with energy, he rolled us over so that I was on the living room rug, and he started play-growling and nipping at my skin, my belly, my breast, my shoulder. He was like a gentle beast, tickling me with his teeth. I giggled. Then he sat up, kneeling with one knee between my thighs and he hollered, "*I love Maddie Richards!*" Then he beat his chest like Tarzan.

I grinned. He looked so handsome, his hair had come loose and it shined like silk in the glow of the naked light bulb. His lips were plump and pink, his eyes shiny with joy. He was rolling in silly.

"I like postcoital Luke," I said.

He pounded his chest again. "I feel like roaring." He collapsed next to me and continued to talk. "Do you ever feel that way? Like you just have so much good inside you that you want to scream it out, share it with the world? Usually, after I orgasm, I just want to go to sleep, but right now, I want to build a fucking fort. Do you want to build a fort?"

"A pillow fort?" I asked.

"Yes. Let's build one and move into it and never come out. I can just live on pussy juice."

"What will I eat?" I asked, feigning innocence.

"Cookies." As soon as the word was out of his mouth, he was moving. He was up, and then he was lifting me, pulling me to his chest so that I had no choice but to wrap my legs around his waist.

I giggle-screamed, "What is happening right now?"

"*We need cookies*." He was yelling like we were trapped in a wind tunnel.

"And I can't walk to the kitchen myself?" I asked, still laughing.

"Nope. You are never taking your legs from around my waist. Never again." He was very matter-of-fact about this. He carried me to the pantry, and balancing me against the wall, he pulled a bag of Milanos out with one hand. After trying to find a way to hold me and the cookies for a second, he made a big show of his ah-ha moment and then held the bag in front of my mouth.

"Am I supposed to carry this with my teeth?" I asked. "Because I could use my hands."

"No, teeth," he confirmed. "This is my cookie expedition. I make the rules." I grabbed the bag between my teeth and play-growled. At the sound, I felt his dick harden against me.

"Shh..." he whispered. Then he pointed to his penis. "He doesn't know about the cookies."

I smiled, letting the cookies drop and get wedged between our bodies. "I don't mind sharing."

"Bedroom, this time?"

I nodded, and we were on the move.

LATER THAT NIGHT, my muscles weighed down by the work of multiple orgasms, I heard him get out of bed. Still groggy, I sat up.

"Are you okay?" I asked, watching him try to tiptoe through the darkness in the bedroom. He was still naked.

He turned back. "I didn't want to wake you. You snore so pretty."

I threw a pillow at him. He quickly shielded his junk with a move reminiscent of *Saturday Night Fever*. Once I stopped laughing, he said, "I want to put my drawings in the truck." He dropped his voice to a whisper. "I'm worried about Mr. Wiggles." He didn't try to cover himself in any way. He was comfortable enough around me to let it all hang out, and that made my insides all bubbly.

I flopped back down, lying on my side, my head propped up with my elbow. "Valid, he could cuddle or knead them to death."

"I'm hoping he hasn't already. But all things considered, if my greatest works are lost to the affections of the cat, it was so worth it."

"Yeah, it was," I boasted. I leaned across the bed and grabbed the unopened cookies from the night table. "We'll be here when you get back. Also, you should probably put on pants."

"Pants, schmants," he said as he walked away.

Happy, I leaned back against my pillows and popped a cookie in my mouth.

"Can we please eat now?" Maddie pleaded, handing me a towel.

I was climbing out of her shower where we had meant to get clean but wound up getting dirty all over again. Maddie's bathroom was little and perfunctory, creamy tiles and brown wood, but like the rest of her house, she made it her own. She painted the walls turquoise and hung little circular black and white cameo paintings that looked like Victorian silhouettes.

"I've got just the thing," I offered, thrusting my hips at her. I was always inclined to be goofy when she was close.

"Oh my God," she rolled her eyes at me. "How can you even suggest that? Aren't you worried it might fall off?"

"Nope," I teased. She looked delectable wrapped in her bright-yellow towel, her tits squished where she tucked the fabric tight around her chest, her shapely legs peeking out the bottom, and her long blue hair darker, almost navy when it was wet. She opened the medicine cabinet and grabbed the toothpaste. Before she could use it, I snapped up her toothbrush.

"Wait, are we going out for breakfast or are we eating something out of your fridge?" I asked.

"I have to eat something, like now," she replied. "All you've given me in the last twelve hours is dick and cookies. And not that I'm complaining, but I'm starving."

"So, I'm gonna vote no on the toothbrushing for at least twenty minutes."

"Is this like a thing?" she asked.

"What if we decide to have orange juice?' I suggested.

"I don't have any orange juice," she said so evenly that I couldn't tell if she was joking or just disagreeing with me for fun.

"You're missing the point."

"No, I see that you are greatly affected by the combo of mint and oranges," she smiled and put down the toothpaste like a cop in a movie lowering his weapon as an act of good faith. "Eat first, brush after. Got it?" She winked at me and headed into her bedroom. I followed her. I wanted to follow her everywhere. She threw her towel on the bed, crossing the room naked. For a second, I considered the reality of fucking again. Would my dick fall off? She took in my lecherous gaze and grabbing her kimono, which was hanging on the side of the cheval mirror in the corner, said, "Food, caveman. Remember?"

Once she covered up, my brain rebooted and I was capable of functioning again. I picked up my jeans and put them on. If she wasn't going to eat naked, neither was I.

In the kitchen, she stood in front of the open refrigerator door, just looking in as if she was studying its contents.

She turned to me. "Cold pizza?"

"Fine," I said. What was that pizza joke? Pizza was like sex, even when it was bad it was pretty good. Considering the current status of our sex life, I'd bet the pizza was gonna be perfect.

She pulled a half-moon wrapped in tinfoil out of the fridge and hugged it to her chest. "I know I told you I love you, but right now, I feel like this pizza is the sexiest thing I've ever seen. Are you jealous?" she taunted.

I nodded. "Babe, I'm jealous of anything that gets anywhere near you." I crossed to the cabinet where I knew her plates were and met her there. She was leaning her ass against the counter. I boxed her in with my body by resting my palms on either side of her. "It's actually a real problem for me. I've secretly been having fistfights with pastries all over town."

"No wonder the muffins at the Conway Cafe seem to cower when I pick up my lunch order." My proximity lowered the tone of her voice. I pinned her hips to the counter with mine and kissed her, not wild but wet. She didn't seem to mind, but she continued to hold tightly to the pizza at her chest. My girl was hungry. I broke from her mouth and opened the cabinet behind her head.

"Water? Coffee?" I asked, pulling a mug down for myself.

"I'll have coffee too," she said, turning to grab the plates and at the same time, rubbing her bottom across my cock. I groaned at the sensation, almost pinning her to the counter again. She ducked under my arm, backing away.

"Sorry," she said, smiling, "I guess I find you a little irresistible."

She took the pizza and the plates to the table and started eating immediately. I wasn't offended. I stayed back and popped a K-cup into her Keurig coffee machine. "I was thinking," I said, not making eye contact. "I want you to meet my family."

She didn't say anything right away because she was chewing. I turned and tried to read her face. Maddie was amazing. She was bold and funny. She was gorgeous and I loved her. But I also thought she felt nervous about my family. It wasn't any one thing she'd done. Maybe it wasn't even her. Maybe it was my interpretation of the ugliness her family had caused in her life. All I knew was that she was private. In some ways, she kept her world small by only ever really being herself with a chosen few. I felt lucky to be on that list.

I leaned back against the counter and waited for her to speak. After she swallowed, she shrugged her shoulders and said, "Okay."

I couldn't contain my joy. "Yeah?" I grinned.

"Sure."

"I think you're going to love them." I carried her coffee to her and went back to start mine.

She shrugged. "I've met your brothers."

I popped the second K-cup in and spoke with my back to her. "Yeah, but it'll be different I think, being my girl."

"Are you going to tell them about how we met, about your art class?"

I had to. I wasn't going to make Maddie lie about how we knew each other. I turned to face her so she could see that I was serious. "Yes. I can tell them with you or maybe before you meet them. Whatever makes you more comfortable. I want to move past that stuff." I crossed to the table and sat down.

"You should," she said with conviction.

"I know. It's ridiculous that I'm hiding this piece of myself. I want them to know that I take my art seriously. I want them to take me seriously." I loved my family and they loved me. I needed to clear the air on this issue. Why was it so hard for me?

"They should."

I nodded and took a bite. Just talking about telling them made me nervous. But this was about Maddie, and they had to know that she mattered most of all. For them to know that, I had to come clean. "I want you to know that I want them to take us seriously, Maddie."

She looked down at her plate. She'd suddenly gone from devouring her pizza to picking at it with her fingers. Maybe I needed to change the subject. We were having so much fun together and now she seemed almost grim.

I reached across the table and took her hand. "You okay?" I asked.

She took a deep breath and looked up at me with a sad smile. "Yeah," she said. But she wasn't. Okay, no more family talk. I had another subject I wanted to broach.

"So…" I said, taking my hand back. "About last night," I said.

She smiled wider. "Are you trying to make me think of sex again?"

"Yes," I said definitively, but I wasn't really. "Well, no."

She pushed out her bottom lip, acting pouty.

I continued. "Actually, I thought we should talk about what happened."

She seemed a little confused. "You're not trying to get me to think about sex but you want to discuss 'what happened' between us during sex?"

I laughed. "No, I want to discuss birth control." Her face fell completely. Maddie went from light and sunny to dark and stormy in one second. I couldn't quite get my mind around the shift, but I tried to manage it anyway. "I mean, don't get me wrong. That was awesome. And if there is a little cooing and pooing result, then I'm all in, but I thought we should discuss…"

She interrupted me. "There isn't."

Now, I was confused. "What do you mean?"

She turned inward and started talking under her breath. "I just wanted today. Couldn't I just have this one day?"

She was scaring me. "Maddie, What's up?"

She stood and started to pace with her arms crossed over her breasts, hugging herself. "I can't," she said, her voice wobbling. She stopped talking and took a breath to re-center herself. "There is no baby now or ever."

I was still confused. "I'm sorry. I don't understand what you're telling me."

She stopped moving completely and yelled at me. "I can't be pregnant. I can't get pregnant. I'm infertile, okay? I starved my ovaries. I damaged them permanently. I'm a fucking barren wasteland."

My stomach sank, and for the first time since my mother died, I thought I might cry. I didn't want this for her. I didn't want this for us. I wanted everything with Maddie, including a family. In an instant, a dream I hadn't fully realized was ripped away. I choked on it, just for a second. Maddie was watching me, evaluating my reaction. I wasn't sure what to say. So, I didn't say anything.

"You should go," she said.

"What?" My tone was aggressive. I felt the heat of anger bubbling under my skin. She was being so irrational. I should go? What in God's name was she talking about? This was a big deal. We needed to talk about it. I stood and moved to her but she stepped back.

"This isn't what you want." She turned, grabbed my gray t-shirt from its discarded place on the couch, and threw it at me.

I caught it. I lost control and yelled, "Maddie, stop."

"It's all over your face," she yelled back. "I want you to go." She was crying now.

"Please." I tried to get close to her again.

This time, with intention, she cut in front of me, grabbed my boots, and headed to the door. Throwing it open, she threw my boots out onto the porch and then took my hat off the hook and threw it too before she screamed, "Get out."

"Fine!" I spat and grabbed my keys from the bowl on the counter. As soon as I crossed the threshold, she slammed the door behind me.

Only then, standing in the sunlight with my shirt and keys in my hands did I really think about what was happening. Maddie couldn't have my babies. Not being able to do that for me broke her and I let it.

I turned around and banged my fists against the door. "Maddie," I hollered. "Maddie, please." No matter how much noise I made, she didn't answer. I pressed my forehead to the door and whispered, "I love you."

16

MADDIE

The day after I threw Luke out, I drove to Claire's house. I didn't call before showing up. To be honest, I didn't know that I was going there. I got in the car and started driving and when I turned off the engine, I was in her driveway. I rang the doorbell and when she answered the door, she took one look at my face and pulled me into her arms. I hadn't lived with Claire in more than five years, but her house was the same as it had always been—nothing special. It was a cookie-cutter house in an uninspired zero lot line community, built in the nineteen-eighties. But it was the only place I ever felt cared for and protected, so for me, it was home.

Claire took me inside and settled me on the couch with a blanket and a pillow. "A guy?" she asked.

I confirmed, nodding my head.

"Do you want to talk about it?"

I looked up at her, blond, older-looking than her thirty-seven years, and shook my head. "Not yet," I said.

She clapped her hands against her legs, stood up, and said, "I'm gonna make us a sandwich. Remote is on the coffee table if you need it."

And that was it. She let me and all my misery infiltrate her life.

Claire's husband died before I met her. He was a Marine. It was friendly fire. I was pretty sure her heartbreak was forever. Sometimes I felt guilty because I knew that if she had been happy and married, she wouldn't have had such a soft spot for me. Her loneliness recognized mine. Other times, I thought all we had was each other. Either way, I was thankful for her.

After that first afternoon on her couch, I decided that I needed more Claire to get over Luke, so I texted in sick to both Rufus and Delores and stayed with Claire for five days. For five days, Claire didn't ask me many questions, if any. She brought me ice cream and put up with my moody music and crying. And then, on day five, she came into her guest room and raised the shades, letting the sunlight in.

"Time to tell me the whole story," she said with her hands on her hips.

I rolled over and covered my face with a pillow, trying to block out the light like a teenager.

"I'm tired of listening to that phone buzz on my kitchen countertop. What the hell is going on, Maddie?"

I pushed myself up so that I was leaning against the headboard and hugged the pillow to my chest. "I fell in love," I said and then started crying.

Claire crawled into bed next to me. "That doesn't sound so bad," she said, her voice laced with consideration for my heart.

"He's so crazy good, but he comes from this big family and it can't work, Claire."

She knew why. "Because you can't give him a family?"

I nodded.

"Did he say that?" she asked. "Or did you tell him that?"

"You should see him with little kids," I whispered, intentionally ignoring her point.

"Science has come a long way. You never know. It might be different now than when they told you that you couldn't have babies."

"He deserves his own family. Little towheads that carry his genes. He'll love them." I wiped the tears from my eyes, growing braver in my decision to push him away.

"I think maybe he loves you."

I stood up. "I'm going to shower."

Claire kept talking. "You deserve love, Maddie. A big giant overwhelming love that fills you to the brim."

I turned to her and smiled weakly. "You do too."

She smirked back. "Touché."

ON DAY SIX, I went home. Claire hugged me goodbye and I promised to come back in a few weeks. On the drive, I called Delores.

She answered the phone by saying, "Oh, thank God. Where are you? I've been so worried. Are you okay?"

I was surprised she was concerned. "I'm fine. I'm sorry I didn't call." I sounded monotone even to myself.

"What did you do to that boy? He is here every day, Maddie."

How embarrassing. I hadn't considered that scenario. I figured that as long as I didn't answer his calls, he'd get the message that there was no solution here. "I'm so sorry, Delores. I didn't mean to bring my drama into the salon."

She laughed. "What is better than drama in a salon? I'm just sorry you're hurting, honey."

"I really don't want to see him."

"He shows up every day, as soon as he's done on the ranch. If you want, I can go out there and run him off for you."

"No, I'll be in tomorrow. I'll take care of it."

Before I hung up, she said, "I can't wait to see you. I know you've only been here for a few months, but this place isn't the same without you now."

Hearing her care, her sentiment that I belonged, I knew I wanted Conway to be my home, but I wondered how I could breathe in the town where Luke would meet someone else, fall in love, and have the babies I could never give him.

I was sitting at the dining table with my family when I received Maddie's text.

It said: *Luke, please stop looking for me at the salon. You are keeping me from doing my job. Also, do not come to my house. If you continue to pursue me, you will force me to permanently leave Conway. I'm sorry. It's better this way.*

I read it five times, trying to picture her writing the words. Tension raced through my body, knotting my muscles from head to toe. What the ever-living fuck? This was how she was signing off? It's better this way? That shit read like I was a stalker, rather than a man who couldn't seem to get through to a woman who he would literally jump in front of a moving train for. Also, who was this fucking robot texting me? Where was Maddie? It was like invasion of the body snatchers. First, she throws me out. I thought we were going to have a fight, not never see or talk to each other again. Then I can't reach her or find her. Thank God, Delores told me she was with Claire. I was out of my mind thinking something happened to her, visions of carbon monoxide poisoning or falling in the shower strangling my every thought. And now, this is what she says?

I get it. I reacted poorly. But honestly, how else was I supposed to react? She told me something sad. Something that hurt. Was I supposed to laugh and be like, *kids, schmids, who wants any of those?* I also get that this is a thing for her. I think she'd been struggling to tell me for a while, but still, we couldn't work through it if we didn't talk about it. She didn't make any room for me to formulate an opinion. I'd had time now. I'd thought about it. And, honestly, there were many options for us. We could try fertility treatments. We could adopt kids. Or we could never ever have any and I would still want Maddie. I had a fucking barrel of siblings. I was probably going to be an uncle a dozen times over, and with no kids in our house, we could spend our lives christening every surface. That sounded awesome. I couldn't tell her that I'd imagined a life where I wasn't a father before I met her, but now I had, and it didn't kill me. A life without Maddie, that was unbreathable.

Fuck that stupid text message. With a scream trapped in my chest, I threw my phone down on the table.

"Whoa there, Patty, who pooped in your sprouts?" Cody asked.

Wyatt chuckled.

"Fuck you both," I spat, my voice bitter with years of repressed anger.

Wyatt's eyebrows shot up, surprised. "Someone, clearly."

"Language, Luke," my father said nonchalantly from the end of the table.

"No. Fuck them. Fuck each and every one of you. I'm a grown-ass man. I'm a vegetarian. Why do you care?" I was loud, shaking with anger. "You know what else? I'm an artist. A good one. And I drive an hour from here to take art classes so that you jerks won't give me a hard time."

Bill tried to speak. "You drive—"

"No. You don't get to say anything yet." I stood up, eyeing each and every one of them. "I'm always the butt of your jokes. Do you know that? I go out there and work our ranch just as hard as any of you and you treat me like the fucking blond sheep of this family." I punctuated my rant by hitting the dining table with my fist. In my head, I'd called myself the blond sheep rather than the black sheep a million times.

Looking around the room, I realized that the color had drained from all my brothers' faces and Sarah looked like she might cry.

My father spoke first. "Sit down, son."

I sat. He was the boss after all, but he was also a constant voice of reason for all of us.

He continued. "Okay, I think we all see that Luke is upset. Am I right?" My siblings all nodded. "Do y'all have things you want to say to him?" His way of mediating felt familiar. It was how he managed us when we were teenagers.

Bill spoke first. "I honestly didn't know we were hurting you, Luke. I'm sorry." My other siblings concurred by nodding their heads.

I put my head in my hands, emotion raging in my chest, tears threatening to spill from my eyes. I didn't know how much anger I was holding back. Without looking at them, I said, "Shit, I didn't mean to yell like that but it's true. It's a death by a thousand cuts kind of thing. I feel like y'all are constantly making me feel like I'm a joke."

"Language," my father said again and my brothers laughed. My father cursed like a sailor but never let up on us using off-color words.

Sarah spoke up. "Can you tell us about the art class?"

God, I'd made such a mess of all this. I was supposed to confess this stuff in a way that was well thought out and now I just screamed it all out like a madman. I took a deep breath. "It's a drawing class," I said, not making eye contact with anyone.

"I remember that horse you drew on the side of the barn before we painted it with Mom," Wyatt said. "Do you remember that, Bill?"

"I do," my father said. "Looked like a living beast, like it was going to run off into the pasture at any moment. Your mother took a million pictures of it the day before we bought the paint."

I don't know why that was the trigger but I started crying, giving them a whole new reason to make fun of me. Only, they didn't. Sarah jumped up from her seat and hugged me.

"Goddammit, I feel terrible. I promise I'll never call you Patty again," Cody said.

I wiped my eyes. "No, you can. It's not that you guys call me Patty. I just need to know that you are behind me, no matter what."

"Fuck, I'd literally die for you, brother," Wyatt said.

My father shook his head, smiling. "What am I going to do about this language?" We all rolled our eyes.

Bill picked up his knife and fork and started to cut his chicken while he spoke. "Okay, so you're taking a drawing class. You said it's an hour from here, so at Fletcher?"

I nodded. The others picked up their silverware, and Sarah returned to her seat.

He continued. "That's cool. What can we do to support you?"

"There's an exhibition next week. I guess you could come." Thinking about class and the exhibition, I wondered if Maddie would be there, and I started blubbering again like a little baby. For the record, I wasn't hysterical. I was just a sappy fuck.

"Oh no," Sarah said, jumping back up. With her arms around me, she said gently, "What's happening now? I feel like this is more than just overwhelming for you."

"Maddie," I managed to choke out.

Sarah stage whispered to the rest of them. "See, I told you they were on the outs."

I looked up at her. She shrugged. "It's a small town."

Of course, they knew.

Sarah shooed Bill out of his seat so that she could sit next to me. "What happened?"

I started from the beginning. I told them all about how Maddie was the model in my drawing class, and how I was crazy about her from the first moment I laid eyes on her. I told them how funny and smart she was and how stupid I was that first day in the salon. I kept the dirty details to myself, but I told them my drawings of her were the most beautiful I'd ever done. Then I told them what she had told me, that she was infertile, and how my reaction scared her and she ran away. I also showed them the text.

Everyone was real quiet when I finished talking, and then Bill said, "Do you love her?"

I nodded. "Absolutely."

"Infertility, that's some heavy shit," Cody said, an undercurrent of uncertainty lingering in his voice.

My father said, "Language," under his breath. No one really listened.

"It is," I said, replying to Cody. "And it isn't. Lots of people get married and face infertility after the fact."

"You getting married?" Bill smiled.

I shrugged. Sarah bit back a giant grin.

I continued. "I have the opportunity to know that this is an issue right now, and to decide that I choose Maddie anyway. I should rephrase that; I want her to choose me. This doesn't make Maddie less. I want Maddie more than I want babies. I'm sure of that."

"And you're sure you won't feel differently a few years from now?" Sarah asked, echoing the sentiments that I was sure Maddie felt.

"I'm sure. If we decided together that we want children, well then, we will find a way. But I don't need children. I need Maddie."

My father asked, "So, she's the one then?"

I nodded again. "No doubt."

"Well, hot shit and holy fuck, we got ourselves a love story," my father beamed. We all laughed.

"See," Bill said, pointing to our dad. "I told you, romantic as they come."

Sarah, whose eyes were rimmed with happy tears, bopped Bill on the arm and said, "Stop it. This is so cool. I'm so excited." She clapped her fingers together.

I rolled my eyes at her. "She won't even talk to me, Sarah."

Wyatt grabbed the mashed potatoes and scooped way more than his fair share onto his plate before he said, "Don't you worry about that. I have a plan." Then he winked at me like he was a freaking genie or something. "Got it covered, bro." He took a big bite of potatoes and smiled around the table at each of us. We all stared at him, waiting for him to explain. Instead, he shook his head and said to himself, "Blond sheep, clever. I have to remember that."

MADDIE

I couldn't keep myself from going to the art show. I kept trying to tell myself that it was about me, that I had spent all these months working on accepting and falling in love with my body and that seeing everyone's drawings of me was part of that process. But was that really true? Deep down, underneath all my bravado about my body love, all I could think about was Luke. Would he be there? Would his family be there? Did he tell them about the class? Or did I screw that up for him too?

The day of the exhibition, Delores offered to do my hair. I never really let anyone do my hair. It was kinda my thing. But I thought being cared for would help me feel less alone.It didn't. As soon as I leaned back into the sink and felt her fingers massage my scalp, I was crying. Delores didn't say anything. She just kept going. Scrubbing and rinsing until it was clean and wet. She wrapped my head in a towel like the Queen of Sheba and when I stood up, she hugged me.

"I'm not gonna push," she said. "But you are not alone, Maddie."

I didn't say anything at first. I wanted to. I walked to Delores' chair and sat. She started by brushing out my hair. I watched her move around me, her eyebrows drawn together in concern, gently pulling and combing, eradicating knots.

"I miss him," I said.

Delores didn't look shocked that I spoke. She took a breath and said, "I'm betting he misses you too. No, I know he does. That boy is grumpin' all over town."

"I love him," I said.

"Funny way of showing it," Delores joked, no judgment in the comment. She turned on the blow-dryer and picked up a round brush.

"I'm protecting him," I said, not making eye contact. Everything about the choices I made felt like they didn't fit. The last couple of weeks without Luke were dark. I had no appetite. I couldn't sleep, and if I did sleep, I woke up looking for him. It was like my soul was shrinking.

"From you?" she asked, not breaking the rhythm of straightening my hair.

I nodded. Then my eyes welled up.

She paused, letting the dryer flop loosely in her hand. "What's wrong with you?" Her voice was sweet and kind and still incredulous, like I was maybe a little stupid.

"I can't have babies." It took all the trust in the world to say these words out loud to Delores. I had only ever told this to Claire and Luke. This was my secret. I hated it. I hated that I broke myself, that I let my parents break me. It was this big ugly rotten scar that I constantly tried to throw a tarp over and drop in a well. Only, it came back. Every time I tried to push it away, it came back. And now, it was taking Luke from me.

"So?" Delores quipped. "What does that have to do with you and Luke?"

I stuttered, "He... I... I can't take that from him."

"First of all, that's his decision. And secondly, he'd be lucky to not have babies with you. I'm overstepping now, but maybe you should talk to him? See how he feels about all this? I'm going to stand behind you whatever you do, but I think that boy loves you more than imaginary future babies."

I shrugged. "Will you come with me tonight, Delores?"

"Wouldn't miss it." She smiled. "But just so you know, if your tits look better than mine, I'm docking your pay."

I PULLED open the door to the gallery. It wasn't really a gallery. It was more like an art exhibition space attached to the library but they called it the gallery. I was wearing my boots and a little red summer dress that had tiny white hearts printed all over it. It had puff sleeves and a low neckline. I looked sexy and sweet in it. Delores had made my hair look good; it was bouncy long curls, similar to if I'd done it myself, only different, and somehow, that felt fresh and fun. After talking to Delores, I was hoping that Luke would be here. I didn't know what the right thing to do was, but I thought she was right; I needed to talk to him.

The setup was what you might expect from a college. A table with a white tablecloth was by the door, with fruit and cheese platters that looked like someone picked them up at Albertsons and oversized bottles of wine that were self-serve, using little clear plastic cocktail glasses. Delores and I each poured ourselves a glass—red for me, white for her.

"Ready to see what you look like nude?" Delores asked.

A brunette in the corner caught my eye. She looked familiar, but I didn't know her and as soon as she saw me see her, she looked away and then turned and ran off in the other direction. I was so nervous about Luke that I hadn't fully considered how other people were going to react to me as the nude model.

There were three rooms. We started in the one closest to us. Rufus was standing in the center of the room. I said hello and introduced him to Delores.

"Madison was an exemplary model," Rufus said to Delores. "Very professional. It shows in the drawings." He walked us over to one on the far wall. "Like this one."

The drawing we approached was of my hand and only my hand. Delores put her hand over her mouth and giggled.

Rufus' head quirked at her. With his stuffiest voice, he said, "Can I ask why you think this is funny?"

"It's not," Delores said around her giggles. "It's just not what I was expecting."

Rufus turned to me. "She was expecting my boobs," I said calmly, and Delores cracked up.

Rufus blushed. "Well, not to worry, miss. I think you'll find that Maddie is depicted from head to toe. And if full nudes are to your liking, there is a particularly lovely drawing in the last room."

"Should I be nervous?" I asked him.

Rufus smiled, something I hadn't really seen him do before, and said, "No, I think you'll be delighted."

When he walked away, Delores said to me, "That guy is a little weird. Thinks he's important, amiright?"

I nodded. "I don't think he's bad though. Just stuffy." We walked into the second room and Anthony was standing in the corner by what I supposed were his drawings. His sister was there too.

He called, "Maddie!" and I strode toward him. "I'm so excited for you to see these. What do you think?"

Anthony had two pieces in the show. One was a still life of flowers in a vase. It was detailed and well executed, definitely something he could be proud of. The second drawing was of me. It was from early on in the semester when I was still draped. Anthony's angle was from over my left shoulder. He had drawn my face in profile, and I was absolutely peaceful-looking. Calm, still, and yet very much alive. I looked happy.

"This is beautiful," Delores said.

"It is," I echoed.

Anthony breathed a sigh of relief. "You really like it?" he asked.

I nodded.

"I'm starting to get it now," Delores said. "The way they see you helps you to re-envision yourself."

I shrugged. "That was the idea."

"Maybe I should model. Do you think I'm the type?" Delores asked no one in particular.

"I'd love to draw you," Anthony said, then he blushed. "Honestly, I want to draw everyone."

Delores and Anthony continued to converse, and without thinking about it, I wandered off to look at the other drawings. There was a crowd in the third room. They all seemed interested in the works on the far wall. They were whispering, a low hum of chatter that hinted at a certain kind of reverence. I made my way in that direction and the people seemed to move aside as I arrived. There were three drawings on the wall. One was my face, as if I was looking in a mirror. The drawing echoed everything I knew about myself. It was in the eyes, all my pain and sorrow but also my hunger for life and all the love I had to give. All it took was one glance to know that this was Luke's work. He was the only one who knew me like this. The only one who studied me long enough to capture not only my likeness but also my soul.

The second drawing was the one Rufus must have been referencing. It was me on my green couch, the night we made love. The night he told me he loved me. And I was nude, very nude, but I was also absolutely free of inhibition.

The drawing was black and white, save for swirls of blue pastel that served to depict my hair, the unruly blue mane of a lioness. There was nothing about looking at my body in that moment that felt sanctimonious or fearful. Through Luke's eyes, I was like a wildflower, free to grow as I pleased and infinitely more beautiful because of my lack of cultivation. He didn't shy away from the creases or bumps or round bits. He seemed to treasure them, highlight them, as if they were the elements that made me hard to look away from.

My chest felt tight and I could feel my pulse picking up speed. The drawings were hard to look at. They reminded me of how happy I felt in his presence, how comfortable and loved I was. I closed my eyes and took a breath before looking at the third. A part of me worried what he drew after I hurt him, after I pushed him away because I wanted to protect him. When I opened my eyes, the image before me was unfathomable.

It was us. Luke and I, only, not now. It was us, older. We were standing with our arms around each other. My head was thrown back in laughter and he was smiling, watching me with such love. There were laugh lines around my mouth and I looked a little rounder. He had gray in his beard and crow's feet at the corners of his eyes. The picture was in full color, my hair was still royal blue and behind us was the rolling green and the big blue sky of Montana. The little white placard on the side of the drawing read:

Luke Morgan

Home Sweet Home, 2020

Pastels

. . .

As soon as I read the title, I gasped and my hands jumped to cover the sound. It was at that moment that I became aware of the utter silence around me.

I sensed him before he said any words. He was directly behind me. Not so close that he could touch me, but close. The room was so quiet that the sound of his voice seemed to dance around me when he spoke. "Maddie?"

I turned before I said anything, and then I was speechless. They were all there, his family. Wyatt and Cody I knew, but also two other men who resembled him, one I assumed was his father, the other his older brother, Bill. The brown-haired girl who had run away from me earlier in the evening was there, and she looked familiar because she had the same eyes as him. That was Sarah, and she was smiling so wide her face must have hurt. Standing next to her was my Claire, who was also smiling and leaning on Delores. They were all behind Luke, standing in a semicircle, looking at me. In front of me, Luke dropped to one knee and tears started to quietly streak down my cheeks.

"Sometimes, you don't know what you want. Like you look at a menu and you could choose any one of the entrees and you'd be perfectly happy, and then there are other times when only one thing will do. This is one of those times for me, Maddie. It doesn't matter what anyone else has to offer, you are the only thing I ever want."

I tried to interrupt him. "But..."

He smiled at me. "I'm not finished." He pulled a ring box from his pocket. "This ring was my mother's. My father gave it to me to give to you. My whole family knows about us; they know our secrets—yours and mine—and they are here to assure you that I want our future, whatever it brings. My father, my brothers, my sister... we all want you to wear my mother's ring and become a part of our family. You are more than enough. You are everything." He paused and cleared his throat. "So, what do you think? You wanna grow old with me?"

I bit my lip, trying to stop the onslaught of emotions from pouring out. He was so beautiful, baring his soul before my family and his. Looking into his eyes, I was afraid that I would fail him, but I wasn't willing to put myself last anymore. Sometimes you have to let someone love you. Sometimes that's what's best for you both.

"Well?" he asked, still smiling but starting to look a little nervous.

"Will there be cookies?" I asked, cheeky until the end.

His eyes lit up. "Truckloads, baby."

"Then, yes."

He stood up, wrapped his arms around me, holding me to his chest, and the audience behind us broke into cheers.

Need more Luke, Maddie, and the rest of the Big Sky Cowboys?
Check out the Big Sky Cowboys Series coming soon on Amazon.

ALSO BY LOLA WEST

Check Out the Big Sky Cowboy Series

Tofu Cowboy

Her Comeback (Oct 2020)

Imperfect Harmony (Nov 2020)

Wild Child (Dec 2020)

Her First Rodeo (Jan 2021)

Hot for the Holidays

Mistletoe in Malibu (Nov 2020)

DID YOU LOVE TOFU COWBOY?

Dear Reader,

I would be ever so grateful if you would take five minutes and write me a review. I want to hear your opinions. Also, good reviews on Bookbub, Goodreads, or Amazon let other people know that mine is a book worth reading. Reviews mean book sales, and sales mean I can continue to write books for you!

Thank you in advance.

XO,

Lola

P.S. You can Click this link to leave and amazon review right now!

ABOUT THE AUTHOR

Lola West writes short, sweet, smart, silly, sexy romance. With a PhD in women's studies and a flair for the dramatic, Lola likes to keep it real. Her loves are cotton candy, astronomy, kitten heels and small-town hunks. Lola's heroes make you swoon and her heroines that talk back. Also, she believes that consent is always sexy, even in books.

You can learn more about Lola by visiting lolawestromance.com and find a **FREE BOOK,** a prequel to the Big Sky Cowboys Series or find her hanging out all over the internet.

Find that you're suddenly a Lola West Fan?
Follow Lola on Instagram
Follow Lola on Facebook
Follow Lola on Goodreads
Follow Lola on Bookbub
Hang with Lola in the private Facebook group:
Sugary Sweet & Lots of Heat

SNEAK PEEK

FALLING FOR THE OPPOSITION (COMING 2021)

DREW

The first time I saw her, she was dancing. No, not just dancing—something else. She was fucking flying, communing with the music like it was in her blood cells, rushing, pushing, flowing through her veins. I was at Bonnaroo—well, sort of. I wasn't sleeping in the dirt, sweaty and camping like she probably was. I was staying in an air-conditioned tour bus and living like a rock star. I was there because it's what you do when you're in college. You drive eleven hours with your rich friends. You leave the pressure of being a senator's son at home. You remind everyone not to take your picture if you're holding a joint, and then you get high and drunk and you listen to the music and make memories that last a lifetime.

When I saw her, it was the final day of the festival, really late in the afternoon, maybe even evening. The sun was dipping low, spilling out all hot and yellow over the horizon. I was in some VIP viewing area, drinking a beer out of a plastic cup, surrounded by guys in khaki shorts with straight-haired blonds swaying in front of them or pressed against their laps. I was drunk. Not ugly, sloppy drunk, but my guard was down. She was maybe 60 feet away—to my left and in front of me—not in VIP. It was stupid hot out. Sticky hot. It didn't stop her though. She was full-on dancing.

She was the opposite of the girls I knew. The girls I knew were linear. They were straight up and down—thin and pretty. They were like porcelain dolls. Small, delicate, dainty girls who wanted to be charming accessories. Girls who made you feel like they didn't sweat, let alone shit. Girls who played tennis and golf and talked about other girls, and clothes, and manicures, and diamonds. Girls who had coming-out parties and wore headbands. Girls who looked like my parents and wanted my parents' life.

She was not linear. She was round, soft, plush—so fleshy. I saw her from behind first. She was wearing jean shorts that were a little too tight so her flesh puckered at the waist, just tight enough that I could see the full cut of her ass as she rocked her hips. Her top was this light-weight sexy hippy girl top. The kind of top that ties behind your neck, and her shoulders were bare, tan, kissed with pink from being in the sun all day. Her dark hair was tied up in a bun, minus some sweaty strands that had escaped and were plastered to her neck. There was a small tattoo or a birthmark behind her ear. I couldn't tell from where I was standing. Her arms stretched above her head, her shoulders rolling to the rhythm of the music. Languid fucking movements. Jesus. When she circled in place so that she was facing me, I finally saw her face. It was as though the music owned her—possessed her features and overwhelmed her. Her eyes were closed and she was biting her lower lip. She also wasn't wearing a bra and she had real tits, big enough that going braless bordered on obscene. A sliver of her round belly was visible at the hem of her shirt.

Watching her made my chest ache, it made my mouth wet, it made my dick hard. I didn't even know who was playing anymore. I wanted to be closer to her. I wanted to be on her. To kneel in the dirt in front of her, cup her ass in my hands, and rest my cheek on her belly. Don't get me wrong, I wanted to do all kinds of things to her and with her, but I had this overwhelming feeling that pressing my face against her hot sweaty body would make me feel calm. I never feel calm. And all of this... watching her, wanting her, it was completely inappropriate because I was standing with my arm around my date for the weekend, Candice Huffington.

When the song ended, I shifted my weight and quickly adjusted myself, hoping no one would notice that I had a raging hard-on. My movements jostled Candice, and she looked up at me, smiling, completely unaware. I attempted to smile back but it didn't quite happen. I was disgusting. I mean, sure, Candice was not my girlfriend. Not even close. She was a girl I met at my parents' country club. She was nice, like all the other blonds in the VIP section. She giggled at my jokes, was concerned I was drinking too much, and wore a strand of white pearls to Bonnaroo. What was up with that? My parents liked her. I liked her. I invited her, with my friends, but I hardly knew her. I'd fucked her though. Just once.

Fuck.

I was disgusting—an animal with no control.

I glanced back to the dancing girl. She had a bag on her shoulder and she was talking to a girl standing next to her.

She told her something and then she moved to leave. I leaned over to get closer to Candice's ear, "I gotta go," I grumbled. Smooth, as usual. Candice looked at me quizzically—her pale eyebrows pinched. I leaned in again, "To the bathroom." She started to gather her things like she was going to come with me. I shook my head. "I'll be right back." She smiled. She always smiled. I was a dick.

I strolled towards the back of the VIP section in the direction of the bathrooms. I could still see the girl making her way through the crowd. She moved quickly and strategically with no fear, owning her trajectory through the hoard as if the seas parted for her. I knew I was going to follow her; that was my intention. The only question was if she would head towards her camp, the restrooms, or the food venues. Obviously, the restrooms would have allowed me to utterly avoid suspicion, but honestly, I didn't care that much either way. When she headed for the food and drink, I barely glanced behind me to see if anyone was watching. Once I got close to her, ten to fifteen feet behind her, I let her set the pace and watched her hips sway as she walked.

It had rained the night before and there was mud everywhere. She didn't swerve to avoid the puddles. She just tromped right through, letting little speckles of dirt stick to her shins and calves. I was glad she wasn't prissy. She didn't look prissy. I followed her lead, my steps sinking each time they hit the muddy ground. She kept her bag close to her hip, holding it with her hand, and I couldn't help but think that it mattered—that whatever was in that bag, money or whatever—she needed it. I didn't know that feeling. Money came easily to me. I was born with it, and I would most likely die with it. Everything I had was replaceable.

She got in line at a stand that sold Philly cheesesteaks and I felt a tinge of joy that she wasn't a vegan or a vegetarian. It's not that there is anything wrong with people who fight for animal's rights or choose vegetables as their mainstay because they think it's healthy. But I didn't want her to be that. I wanted her to be untethered, wild, and vast, just like her dancing. I didn't want her to be clean or fearful. I wanted her to be greasy and rich. I wanted her to be danger-ous. I wanted her to skydive. I wanted her to be the girl who sits on the railing of the balcony on the hundredth floor, the girl who jumps with you—not before or after you. I wanted her to be gluttonous.

I lingered back a bit, glancing about to make it look like I was undecided about what to eat. I was really wondering if I should get in line behind her. I didn't feel all that hungry, but the smell of the sizzling meat wasn't unappealing. Normally, with any other girl, I would have engaged sooner, but with this girl, I kept wondering how you feel about the guy that hits on you when you're in line for a cheesesteak? Do you think that guy is a turd? What if his breath smells of beer and other sundries? Are you repulsed by him?

Frozen by anxiety, I let myself watch her again. From where I was standing, I could see that the markings behind her ear were a tattoo. Small and unobtrusive, a constellation of asterisks. She looked around, scanning the crowd as if she was searching for someone. Who? An icy tightness constricted my chest. I considered that she might be waiting for a guy. Her boyfriend? Sheer jealousy propelled me forward. I crossed from where I was standing to get in line behind her. From this close, I could smell her. Three days baking in the hot sun wasn't good for anyone, but her odor wasn't rank. She was musky, earthy like the woods, a simple, soft human scent that made me want her more.

There were three people ahead of us, but for me, they weren't people. They were increments of time. Each person represented maybe a few minutes, which meant, best-case scenario, I had nine minutes to make an impact. Nine minutes to get her to notice me. Nine minutes to strike up a conversation so valuable that she would want me. Or at the very least, nine minutes to earn myself a tenth minute. She continued scanning the crowd. She looked over her shoulder... in my direction. It was my opening. No gimmicks, just conversation. Deep breath.

I looked right at her, the words about to drip from my tongue, and then I saw recognition in her eyes. She pressed up on her tip-toes, waving her hand in the air, bouncing. Oh, God—tits. I didn't want to embarrass myself by having her first exchange with me be my eyes molesting her, so I looked at my feet.

"Joe! Joe!" she hollered, still waving frantically. A very tall gangly guy with a neatly trimmed beard and mirrored aviator sunglasses brushed past me. He was good looking in a grungy, fashion-y way. Not great looking, but man enough. His arms wrapped around her and he lifted her from the ground. She wrapped her thighs around his waist, squeezing her whole body against him.

"God, I missed you," she cooed, and I tasted vomit at the back of my throat. She was supposed to be mine, but apparently, I didn't have nine minutes. I didn't have any minutes. She already belonged to some dude with shaggy chestnut hair and leather bracelets. I lingered for a moment, gnawing the inside of my cheek. He released her, returning her to the ground but continuing to hold her hand. Once they turned their attention to what they were going to order and share, I fucked off.

I strolled through the crowd in the direction of the camp-grounds. There were people everywhere and it was an eclectic group. Lots of regulars—everything from preppy frat boy types like me to hippie types like her, but there were also crazy motherfuckers. People covered in neon paint. People in full-feathered Native American headdresses. People on stilts. People in tutus and sailor costumes. I hated them all. I wanted to snarl, to growl. I wanted to be rabid. My brow furrowed and I clenched my fists. I needed to break something. Fuck someone up... get fucked up... get fucked... something. What I really wanted was to punch my fist into his neatly trimmed jaw and watch the impact in slow motion like you do in the movies. I wanted to see his whole face crumple as if it was going to permanently lose its shape. I wanted to see the blood on his lips, the shock and awe in his eyes. I wanted him to be afraid of me. I wanted him to piss himself when people said my name. But that shit was way the fuck out of proportion, considering I'd never even spoken to her.

So, I tried to breathe. I leaned my back against a tree and then let myself slide down until my ass hit the ground. I rested my elbows on my knees and held my head in my hands. The ache that claws at your face right before you cry crept into my cheeks. I closed my eyes and pressed my palms against them. I swallowed and sucked the emotion down. There was no way I would go all weak over some hippy chick that I'd never even spoken to—no way. I thought about going back to VIP. Candice was probably wandering around looking for me. I could go back to her.

She'd let me fuck her again. I knew she would, but I didn't want to. Fucking Candice was cold. She spread her legs and welcomed me and she made enough noise to seem like she wanted me, but her eyes were empty. Fucking Candice was a lie. A dirty lie. Candice wanted to be the girl dating the senator's son. Going back to Candice wasn't an option. So, I just sat there until it was really dark out.

After a while, a group of geeky looking assholes congregated around one of those one-piece benches and a picnic table that was off to my left. I could see them because they had a lantern, but I was pretty sure they couldn't see me. There were five of them, but one stood out as their leader. He was a boney dude with hard, thin features. He looked crooked—gnarly, like a kid who wore a trench coat to high school. A kid no one liked. Or maybe a kid whose life's mission was to hack into the CIA. He didn't look like a good kid, but not bad either—just unwanted. The others were also variations on this theme. They looked like dudes that loved girls who played video games.

They were smoking cigarettes. I didn't smoke, but it seemed like something to do, so I got to my feet. These kinds of guys weren't usually down with the likes of me. I was too clean-cut for their tastes. I reminded them of the footballer who gave it to their girlfriends in high school. I reminded them of the money their parents didn't have. I was that bullshit jock, that asshole frat boy who had it easy, who didn't know what it meant to survive on the outside. They didn't know shit. For most of us, there was no inside, no in-crowd. We were always alone. Always unsure and unsupported—following all the rules because we didn't have a choice. But it didn't matter. Not to punks like this, and honestly, I deserved their hate. I had done it all—pissed in their water bottles, thrown them in dumpsters, taken their little sisters' virginity, all to be cool.

Still, I approached them—cocky, smirking. I wanted to feel the rush of control. I wanted to eat their discomfort. Their conversation halted as I hoisted myself onto the table and rested my feet on the bench. They smelled homeless, but after three days in the mud, the dancing girl was the only one who didn't.

"What's up, dudes?" I tossed the words at them. My voice was steady and deep, overly confident.

A small guy with acne and spikey hair at the end of the table rolled his eyes, and the leader who was sitting with his hands on the table by my hip shook his head, raised his eyebrows in sarcasm, and said, "Not much, man. Can we help you?" It wasn't a warm and fuzzy welcome, but I didn't want it to be.

"Oh, ya know," I jostled his shoulder and felt him tense up, "I was just sitting over there enjoying the fanfare when, suddenly, I had an undeniable craving for a smoke, and well, wouldn't you know? Here you are... smoking." I smiled a tight-lipped smile.

He glanced at his friends. I noticed his hair was greasy and felt the rumble of something secret. Something they knew and I didn't, but I didn't care that much. He looked back at me, crossed his arms over his chest, and smiled the smile of a trickster—curled lips, all teeth. "Sure, dude. Twenty bucks." He said it casually. No fear. I had no power over him.

"Twenty bucks?"

"Yeah, man. Cigarettes are precious cargo in this joint. And honestly, I'd rather give them to hot chicks than to you." He pulled the pack out of his pocket and tapped it against his palm. He had a long angular nose that was crooked like the rest of him. "So, if you really want one, you're gonna have to pay for it."

"Fuck you, man. That's sexist." The geek chuckled, and for a split second, we were friends. I sighed and shook my head as I pulled my wallet out and handed the guy a twenty. "Plenty more where that came from, right?" Smirk, our friendship ended.

He scowled at me and tugged a cigarette from the pack. I took it. "You want a light?" he asked. Instead of answering, I bent towards him, cupping my hands to protect the lighter from the wind, which had picked up a touch since the sun went down. It took a couple of tries for the lighter to catch. It didn't bother me. I liked the zippering sound of the flint wheel. Eventually, the flame glowed hot and I sucked in air, igniting the cherry tip of the cigarette.

I knew immediately. My very first drag was like acid. It burned my throat and smelled like gasoline. But I couldn't be the loser twice in one day. So, I stood up, took a second drag, exhaled, and said, "Thanks for, nothin', dude."

I had been drinking and smoking weed all day—that plus whatever those assholes doped me with was a lethal combo. I started to get dizzy a few minutes after I walked away. It seemed like everything around me started to speed up while I slowed down. I walked into people. Colors raced by me, blurring my vision. I was hot, really hot. I pulled my polo shirt over my head and when the air hit my chest, I freaked out. I thought I was naked. I felt the air on my balls. But, when I looked down, I was still wearing my shorts. People near me were talking and laughing and their voices were shrill. I tried to cover my ears, but I could still hear them. The anger from earlier started to percolate under my skin, and I clawed at my own chest. I had to get away from these people, but they were everywhere. I thought of the tree from earlier. I thought of Candice. I thought of the girl. I wanted the girl. I remembered stumbling along looking for her—and then there was nothing for a while.

Well, not nothing. Shards of something, but nothing decipherable. So many sounds, but more than anything, flashes of moments—frozen images in time. Bodies, sweaty and swaying to the music. Someone dancing with a glow stick. A paper plate on the ground. Blood all over my hands. Water spilling over my face and shoulders. The moon. Vomiting. The moon again.

Finally, clarity started to descend. I was on the ground. My neck and shoulders were cricked funny and I had a skull-bending headache. I heard laughing. Something tickled my abdomen. The acrid smell of vomit filled my nostrils. And there was throbbing. My hands were throbbing. More laughter. And voices.

"On his face?"

"Totally, man."

"What should I write?"

"Ass"

"No, Dickhead."

Something fluttered against my forehead—the same tickle I had felt on my abs. It was calming, like when my mom tickled my back when I was a kid. More laughter and clicking. Clicking? No, a shuttering. My brain rattled. I knew the shuttering sound but couldn't place it. It was a bad sound. The shuttering was a camera phone. Whoever they were, they were taking pictures. I tried to open my eyes—but it felt like they were glued shut.

There was a new voice. She was angry, "What's wrong with you?"

"Just harmless fun," one of the voices sneered.

"This is what you call fun? Degrading another human being?"

"Whatever." I could sense eyes rolling. I would have done the same if I ran into the goody-two-shoes who was currently acting as my savior.

"I have an idea, why don't you take your fun elsewhere before I call the cops!" Her tone was unwavering; there was nothing empty about her threat.

"We would be long gone before they got here," a different voice chided.

"Okay, no problem. Let's test your theory." And then I heard dialing.

"Bitch!" someone spat, but they were moving away, feet shuffling.

I pushed myself to stir. A girl I'd once dated—Molly? Meghan, maybe? I couldn't remember. Pretty though, a strawberry blond—curtains matched the drapes, if you know what I mean. Anyway, she had made me go to a yoga class with her, and the teacher's instruction came to mind,

"Slowly, very slowly, bring life back into the tips of your fingers and the end of your toes. Circle your wrists—your elbows, awaken your knees, your calves—and when you're ready, roll onto your right side into a fetal position. This is a safe space—a position that nurtured you for nine months. Finally, with great care, come to a seated position." Her voice had been so calm. One of the most calming sounds I ever heard, but when I broke up with that girl, I never went to yoga again.

My body felt heavy, unruly, but I managed to sit up, and when I opened my eyes, the dancing girl was squatted in front of me. It was almost dawn, so the light was funny and my vision was blurry. I shook my head, thinking maybe I was imagining her—placing her face over the actual woman who had come to my rescue. But when I opened my eyes again, it was still her face, her pouty fat lips, her big dark eyes full of concern. Embarrassment caught in my throat, and I couldn't speak.

"You okay?" she asked, her voice soft, even calmer than the yoga instructor. I nodded. "You want water?" I nodded again. She opened her bag and pulled out a water bottle. It was her water bottle, not a disposable one. She handed it to me. I wrapped my fingers around it. I was slow and uncoordinated. My body felt swollen, like it was made of bread dough. I sucked hungrily at the bottle's plastic nipple, and when I returned it to her, it was almost empty. She didn't seem phased. She just took it from me and put it back in her bag. "I'm gonna find you help. Don't move." She started to stand.

My embarrassment quickly obliterated, replaced by panic. It didn't matter that Bonnaroo had a "No Questions Asked" policy, a senator's son doesn't show up at the medical tent. Period. Before she was standing, I managed a hoarse, "No." She squatted again and looked at me quizzically.

"No?" Her voice had a very physical presence—a right-eousness—like a solider.

"No," I said again, this time stronger.

"You can't get in trouble," she argued more gently, touching my leg. Her touch exploded on my skin, rippling aftershocks up my thigh and into my chest.

"I'm fine." I shifted and attempted to stand, but I was weak and she had to help me to my feet.

"You're not fine. You don't look fine. That hand looks bad." She nodded in the direction of my left hand. It was black and blue in a couple of places, pretty swollen, and there was crusty brown blood on all my knuckles. I had punched something. Hard.

"It's fine." She was not convinced. "Thank you," I mumbled. She looked at me, searching my face, trying to understand my behavior. There was nothing else to say. How could I have her now? Who would want the guy that stood in front of her? She was still looking right at me. Still searching my face, her hands still on me from when she helped me up. I shifted my weight backwards and she dropped her hands. I cleared my throat, tried to smile, and said, "Really, thanks." She nodded. *Goodbye, dancing girl.* I turned and started walking slowly in the direction of my tour bus. I could hear that she hadn't moved, but I didn't look back.

"Wait," she called out. I stood still, but I didn't turn around. She jogged over and stopped so that she was once again standing in front of me, facing me. There was something in her eyes that I was unfamiliar with—something decent. She opened her bag again, took out a green bandana, and poured the last gulps of water from her water bottle onto it. She then braced her left hand against my temple and used her right hand to rub the wet bandana against my forehead. She was trying to wipe away the vandalism—trying to make it so what happened to me wouldn't be so visible. I wanted to cry. At first, she wiped gently. Worry filled her face, scrunching her features. She pressed deeper—rubbing hard.

"It's permanent marker," she sighed. I looked away, swallowed, and looked back.

"You reap what you sow, right?" I meant it as a joke but it came out wrong. It wasn't snide, it was sorrowful.

She searched my face again, and then to my surprise, she hugged me. I was tense at first but when she didn't let go, I relaxed into her. I was so exhausted but not because some assholes doped me or because I had the word "dickhead" scrawled across my forehead or even because she had a boyfriend. I was exhausted because I spent so much time trying to get it right, trying to be the son my father wanted. Her head rested against my bare chest and just like I thought—me against her and her against me—it was like a salve. It was like the bronchia in my lungs were truly functioning for the first time—like I'd never taken a real breath before. Everything in my body relaxed. I pushed my nose into her hair and pulled her tighter to me. My heart was pounding against her ear. It was too much—too raw, too real. I bit my lip hard.

When we separated, she reached up and ran the back of her hand across my jawline. It was personal. Intimate. She was kind. I mattered, and she didn't even know me. "Maybe, you're right," she said softly like we were kissing. "Maybe you reap what you sow or maybe the world is just full of assholes." When she dropped her hand, I knew for sure. I could never have this girl and not because she had a boyfriend. This girl was bigger than me. She was better than me. I didn't deserve this girl.

I stepped back. If I couldn't have her, I had to get away from her. "I gotta go." The words came out hard, cruel even. I tried to soften it, "I... um... I'm sure my buddies are wondering where I am."

"I could help you back to your site?" she offered.

"No, I got it. I'm good."

She offered me the bandana, "To cover your head?"

"It's okay. It's fine." I deserved to be branded even if she didn't want me to be.

She pushed the bandana into my hand. "Just take it."

I did. I stuffed it into my pocket. I wasn't going to argue with her. I stepped to the side, preparing to walk away, but then it occurred to me that I would never see her again and I didn't even know her name. I had to touch her one more time. I wanted to kiss her, but I couldn't, so I grabbed her waist, pulled her to me, pressing my lips against her neck. The tone between us shifted quickly. A tiny shudder escaped her lips. I didn't expect it, and I reacted before I could think, shifting my lips, taking her earlobe between my teeth and pressing my thigh between her legs. The second shudder was deeper—more of a growl. I growled back. My own sound shook me. There was heat coming off her and I wanted so much to absorb it, to run my hand up her thigh and slip my fingers deep into her wetness, to make her shudder over and over again until there was nothing left. But, I couldn't. I wasn't going to take this girl and poison her with my shit. I wanted to know that I had left this girl intact. I wanted to know that she was out there—that something good, something whole and normal existed.

"Fuck..." I pulled back, ran my hand through my hair, then started backing away, still facing her. "I'm sorry... God, I'm so sorry." I was shaking. She just stood there. She didn't smile or try to play it off like it was alright. She didn't say anything. She just watched me. She looked sad, her face still. I turned and kept walking. I walked straight across the site. I passed through the campgrounds and didn't stop to take a breath until I was standing beneath the Ferris wheel; it was turned off so it felt creepy like a ghost town or a post-apocalyptic world. It wasn't really light out yet and everything, everywhere was still. I pulled the green bandana from my pocket, held it to my nose and wished it to smell like her, but it didn't.

When I got back to the tour bus, there was a sock duct-taped to the door and my buddy, Pete, was sitting on the ground. I'd known Pete most of my life. His dad was a corporate lobbyist for big oil, so we were both prep school brats together in DC. We didn't mean to go to the same college, but it ended up that way, and then it was like a done deal— same frat, same friends, lifers. People often thought we were brothers, even though we really didn't look alike. Pete was blond with brown eyes and brown facial hair. I had dark hair and green eyes, but we were built similarly, tall, athletic

—nothing that says obsessive bodybuilder, but nothing that says couch potato either. Pete was just my family and people could tell. He was the guy I'd call if I needed help getting rid of a body.

"Jesus, Drew! What the fuck, man? Where have you been?" He was never one to pull punches, and I respected him for it.

I didn't have an answer. I didn't want to talk about what happened, so I rubbed my face with my hand for a second and then asked, "Where's Candice?"

Pete nodded towards his Land Rover. "Sleeping with Kate." Katie Sullivan was our third. We grew up with her too. She was a year younger than us and an athlete who could whip both our asses in all things, particularly tennis. I swear, if she could have pledged our frat, she would have, just to remind us who was boss. She was good—oddly stiff and very controlled, but good. "She's pissed, dude."

"Candice?"

"No, man. That one is like all worried and shit. Katie's pissed. She's more familiar with your..." He paused, searching for the right words. "Shall we say, extracurricular behaviors." Our whole life, Pete made a constant joke out of the PR spin machine that was my life. "She had to take care of Candice all night. It was not cool, dude." He paused, smirked, and pointed towards my face, "Although, I think that shit on your forehead might help your case a little..." He snickered.

"What's with the sock?"

"Conner."

Conner was the other friend we'd come to Bonnaroo with. He was also in our fraternity. Pete and I had met him as pledges. We trusted him because when we were pledging, he was always the brother who stepped in when he felt shit was going too far. He was a funny guy, the kind of guy everyone liked—the ladies included. The whole ride down from DC, Conner kept making "If the tour bus is a-rockin', don't come a-knockin'" jokes, and apparently, he wasn't kidding. I sat down next to Pete and leaned against the bus. He looked at me with a serious expression. "You look like shit, dude. You okay?"

I nodded and then we were quiet. Pete always seemed to know when to be still and when to push. The bus door inched opened and a petite olive-skinned girl with black hair emerged. She was moving very slowly, stealthily, sneaking out. Pete and I watched her. She looked disheveled, there was a red lipstick stain around her mouth and her mascara had smeared and run. I realized that we needed to say something or else we were going to startle her.

"Hey," I said quietly. The girl jumped, dropping the bus door so that it slammed. So much for not surprising her. She looked at Pete and me for a split second, then ran off in the direction of the other campgrounds. A groggy Conner appeared in her place, hollering after her, "What? No breakfast?"

We laughed.

And then it was time to go. Time to pack up the Land Rover and leave the dancing girl behind.

LUA

Joe, my best friend, is basically a stubborn asshat. As usual, I was standing at his bedroom door waiting for him to be "decent," which, for any normal human being means dressed—like clothed—like not naked. For Joe, "decent" means fashionable, which he pronounces fah-shun-ah-ble; I think the pronunciation is similar to saying tar-jay instead of target, in other words, trying to make something seem like more than it really is... but that's Joe. He's obsessed with living a life that's explosive, and when that's your bag, that's your bag. We've all got to dance to the beat that suits us, but Joe's version is wow. Just wow. To be clear, explosive is not my calling. I like my life soft, rich, and kind, like folk songs, or blurry and wish-filled like a full moon right before it snows. Conversely, I also appreciate practical and useful, so fah-shun-ah-ble is not me, mostly because it takes a lot more time than "decent."

Historically, I would have chosen to just stand there and sigh, waiting for Joe, but I've been impatient lately. And, for Christ's sake, I was wearing a hand-me-down bathing suit and a ratty old beach towel. This was not an instance that required showboating. The plan was to go to the lake. The lake on OUR property. My dad and Joe's parents were founding members of an intentional community—a commune called Community Thrives. We call it the "thrive," and Joe and I have literally lived on the property our entire lives. So, I could pretty much guarantee that Joe wasn't going to run into the love of his life or a modeling scout on the way to the lake. In fact, it was a million times more likely that he'd run into someone who changed his diapers, and honestly, pretty much any outfit is a step-up from poop in your pants.

"JOE!" I hollered, lifting my hands to bang my fists against his door, but instead, I almost fell into him as he threw it open.

Immediately, his hands and chin dramatically rose towards the heavens and he deeply growled, "Patience, Padawan." His vibe came off more Gandalf from *Lord of the Rings* than Jedi knight, but whatever. He was wearing a black t-shirt and a hot pink banana hammock. Not kidding. I rolled my eyes and smiled because he's an asshat, but he's my asshat and I love him. Once he'd cleared his bedroom, aka, his dressing room, he pushed past me, heading for the kitchen. I turned to follow him, noticing that the butt of his itsy-bitsy swim-suit said, *Bootylicious* in stenciled font. There is no question —he ironed those letters on himself.

In Joe's house, the kitchen is actually a great room, very open concept, which is pretty normal for the thrive because we build our own houses, so less walls means less work. Basically, the room is a huge rectangle divided by a counter/breakfast bar type thing that has three wooden stools to go with it. I've eaten more snacks and breakfasts there than I could possibly count. The walls of the room are mud—adobe-like, and Susan, Joe's mom, has painted murals on them—big winding green vines. To the right side of the counter, there are all the things one finds in any kitchen, and to the left, there is a living room/art room/office, featuring an easel, craft table, desk, and a set of mismatched couches and chairs—which are all covered with Afghans and Navajo blankets. In the corner on the far-right side of the room, there is a fireplace and around the hearth are painted handprints of all kids born on the thrive —starting with Joe and I on the bottom left corner. It's homey and comfortable and might just be the place that I have laughed the most in my life.

Like the diva that he is, Joe headed straight to the kitchen, pulled out his air guitar, and belted out a blues-y song of his own making to his mom who was sitting at the kitchen counter reviewing papers, "Good morning, mama. Dodododododo," he whipped his dark hair around and squinted at her. "I don't know if you noticed, dodododododo." Full body toss, followed by squealing, "I oversle-ept." The guitar disappeared and he was creeping toward her with sultry eyes and whispered singing that crescendoed to all-out madness, "Oh, tell me, mama... Tell me! Tell me you packed our lunch. Dodododododo. Because Lua seems oh sooooooo tigh-iiiii-t-ly wound."

Joe's song barely earned a glance up from whatever Susan was working on. Pencil in hand and eyes still on the page, she said, "Joe-Joe, give Lua a break. Going off to college is stressful, kiddo."

Joe and I had completed our AAs, and starting in September, I had a full ride to Hamilton to finish my BA. I was a little freaked out. Okay—a lot freaked out. And Joe was not helping.

"Boooooo," Joe retaliated, heading for the refrigerator door. "Boo! Boo! Boo! I don't think she should get to act all Grumpy McGrump Pants just because she chose to run away to one of the country's bastions of higher learning, binge drinking, and one night stands." He pulled the door open and leaned fully into the fridge, bending at the waist, so from where I was standing, leaning against the doorframe, he was all legs and a full moon of pink bootyliciousness rising. "Gotta make choices you can live with. Right, mom? Isn't that what you taught us?" He didn't pause for an answer. "What do we want for munchies, Lua-cake? Are we thinking light and luscious—like apples and honey, bebe? Ou... deh-cay-dent? Maybe a little wine and cheese?"

"Cheese." Given the option, I'm always going to go cheese.

He finally stood and turned to me. His hands—arms really —were full, goodies tucked tightly against his chest, using his elbows and armpits as pins.

"Just cheese? Please. Where is the charm, mon cheri? The x-peer-ee-ance." Maybe he just likes to make English words sound French. He smiled, all goofy and toothy, "If all I'm doing today is basking in the sun at the lake, then you better believe I'm preparing a foodgasm."

It took him twenty minutes to pack lunch, and by the time we started the hike out to the lake, the sun was set to broil. I didn't mind so much. There is something about a hot summer day that makes me feel connected to everything. It's like my sweat reminds me that I'm just another animal—one of many that sun could fry up quick—and the thrive is so beautiful in the summer. Everything seems to be alive. So green and humid and buzzing.

It's not a terribly long walk, but to get to the lake, we had to go from Joe's house past the central meeting house and the farming fields and then up an uncultivated hill and through the trees. Basically, we had to traverse the entire 350-acre property from one end to the other. We walked in silence. At first, there were ambient sounds—the hellos from other thrivers in their gardens or through their windows, the tractor engine, kids playing, and then as we got closer to the lake, the only sound was the scratching of the tall grass along our thighs and the bottom of the picnic basket.

As you can imagine, Joe doesn't do silence that often, but in this instance, he did it for me and I knew it. He gave me quiet. He gifts me silence whenever he thinks I need to breathe deep and think. He'd been giving me a lot of quiet lately. He thought I needed to come to terms with leaving the thrive and going to college.

It made sense that Joe thought college was freaking me out. When you grow up like we did, the mainstream doesn't exactly make sense to you. It's not what it sounds like. I'm not a freakish loser or incapable of meshing with society. I wasn't raised by wolves, and we didn't grow up in a cult or anything. The thrive is an experiment—a community of people with like-minded ideas. In this case, equality, justice, freedom, care, and community support. Our parents and the other thrivers decided to live their ideals by separating themselves from the grid and everything that comes with it. We grow our own food; we have a community school; we help our neighbors when they can't make ends meet. It's like a huge open-minded family who lives together and spends their free time fighting for equality in the larger world.

I'm proud that I was raised this way. I'm proud of who I am because of it. I mean, I was at my first LGBTQ Pride parade before I could walk. I've protested sexism, racism, ableism, classism... when it comes to human equality, I am there. I have carried a picket sign on the Washington Mall more times than I can count, and I most definitely have an FBI file. Growing up on the thrive is special. It makes you self-sufficient. I can fix a transmission. I can build a shelter. I can grow plants for eating and for healing. I can recite poetry and play the guitar. In the mainstream, I'm a renaissance woman. On the thrive, I'm normal.

But the thrive also makes you a total weirdo once you're old enough to join the mainstream, which for both Joe and I was when we started classes at the local community college. We were the first of our tribe—so to speak—to get old enough to need to go to school outside the commune. Can you say culture shock? I mean, neither Joe nor I saw a television until we were in our late teens, and even then, it wasn't like we had one in our houses. When we began our collegiate journey, our entire community of one hundred and fifty-three people had seven computers and one building with Wi-Fi. Sure, we knew all the best campfire songs, had a well-rounded knowledge of feminist theory, and could raise our own livestock, but we'd never heard of a text message.

The learning curve was fierce. We made mistakes. We thought people our age would understand our perspectives, our openness, our sense of community, and our belief in equality for everyone. We had weird clothes. We hummed and whistled. We thought that the average college freshman would want to talk about Sartre and Simone de Beauvoir. There was some bullying—particularly once people realized we were from the thrive. And then there was also a lot of condescension from so many, including our professors. We would try to explain that computer access was complicated or that we didn't have personal emails or phone numbers and people just looked at us like we were crazy. Eventually, we convinced our parents that any child of the thrive that chose the college route needed a smartphone, a laptop, and access to Wi-Fi. Joe and I also host this whole "intro to college" party every semester to try to prepare the others, but it's still a struggle.

So, yeah, Joe thought I was freaked out about going to college because I'd have to start over and be the weirdo again—which was true, and when I got around to thinking about that, I felt totally freaked out. For sure. But honestly, since Bonnaroo, I wasn't thinking about that. Instead, I was fixated on the guy. I hadn't really told Joe about him, which was weird because I told Joe everything. Well, I did tell him that there was a guy who was out of it from drugs or something and I tried to help him, but I kind of left out the whole moody seduction, soaked panties thing. It wasn't that I wanted to keep it a secret—although, on some level, I was completely mortified. Honestly, it was just that my obsession with the guy from Bonnaroo was effed-up and I wasn't ready to admit that out loud to anyone.

I knew it though. I knew that I was obsessed with some nameless guy. A nameless guy with incredible shoulders, huge grabby man hands, and really good hair, but nameless all the same. From the minute I saw those jerks tormenting him, it was like I had lost my mind. First of all, I know the statistics. I am well versed in the reality that young men, particularly in groups, are not to be trifled with—and this is even more so when you're a woman, alone. And yet, I couldn't stop myself. It was like I was possessed by the ferocity of Shakespeare's Lady Macbeth: "Screw your courage to the sticking place!" I think I would have killed them—those jerks who were tormenting him, clawed their eyes out with my fists and teeth.

Literally, I couldn't remember another time in my life where I went all super mama lion on anyone. I was a pacifist for Christ's sake. I had a vegetable garden and read the works of Mahatma Gandhi. I bought hook line and sinker into the slogan, "make love not war," but in that one moment, I was willing to do anything to stop them. I didn't even consider what they could have done to me. I just jumped. Walked right into the fire with him—and strangely, I was proud of what I did. I felt the rightness of it deep in my intestines. Admittedly, I didn't bite off any earlobes or pull out any fingernails. I squelched the situation peacefully, but I knew that if my "negotiation tactics" failed, I would have devolved into something violent, and for some illogical reason, I couldn't bring myself to begin to feel any shame about that.

Furthermore, and I hate it when people refer to themselves in the third person, but honestly, Lua Steinbeck does not make out with strangers that she found passed out in the dirt. Next to his vomit, I might add. Gross. And yet, when I closed my eyes, I could still feel his hands on me. With no rhyme or reason, my mind drifts to my moments with him —the expanse of emotion that flashed in his eyes when he blamed himself, the heat of his chest against my face, his aching gaze as my hand touched his jaw, the flutter of his lips against my neck, the explosion of desire as his mouth found my ear, and *oh, God...* those few seconds when he crushed my body against him and rolled my hips so that everything hard and soft about us caught fire. This memory just flared up and repeated on me like I was a skipping CD —trapped in some cosmic game of infinite repeat. Honestly, it didn't matter where I was or what I was doing. I was constantly plagued by the feeling of him. It was a visceral need. I ached for him, a stranger who had "dickhead" scrawled on his forehead when I met him and never actually kissed me—like lips to lips. EFFED-up.

The worst part about my endless distraction was that I knew nothing. Literal dickhead guy could be anywhere... anyone. The likelihood of us crossing paths again was slim, a million to one, more, a needle in a haystack, a galaxy in the universe, a singular atom in the wide Sargasso Sea, and yet, I thought I'd see him again, which is ridiculous—as absurd as Joe's swimsuit. Inane. Ridiculous and downright juvenile. And somehow, I still felt all romantic-y, which made me want to vomit. Destiny was not something I bought into and soul mates, please. I had things to do—college to prepare for. I couldn't constantly be drifting off into the land of unrequited orgasms and achingly sexy sorrowful eyes.

And so, instead of sharing, I was silently walking with Joe who seemed to be getting huffy. He started making sounds —sighs and grunts of aggravation. In just a few more steps, we'd be able to see the lake and he wanted me to talk to him. This was part of our friendship. Joe gives me just enough space to think and then he forces me to talk. When we broke through the tree line, Joe dropped the picnic basket and started running.

He pulled his shirt off as he went, and once he'd discarded it, he turned so he was facing me, and running backwards, hollered, "Last one in has to tell the whole truth and nothing but the truth." He'd cheated. There was no chance that I'd catch him before he hit the water, but that was the point. I quickly dropped the towel and tore off after him.

The water was dark—cool and green, exactly how a lake is meant to be. We'd been acting like goofy kids, splashing and ducking each other for at least fifteen minutes before Joe swam towards the shore and situated himself so that he was sitting Indian-style in about a foot of water. I stayed out where it was waist-deep, not wanting to spill my guts just yet. He beckoned to me, "Come on in, Lua."

"Not quite ready yet," I whined.

"Fine. Be a petulant child. The longer you stay out there, the more time I have to truly appreciate your rack."

He was teasing me. Forcing me to swim in and silence him.

"I mean, that is a shitty swimsuit and still your tits are perfect."

I was on the move. "Cut it out, Joe." As it got shallower, I moved faster, planning to dive at him.

"Honestly, you are so gorgeous—all round and deliciously fleshy—it's just too bad your snatch is—"

He didn't get to finish because I clobbered him with my full body weight and pinned my hand across his mouth.

"My snatch is what, Joe? Huh? What nasty thing were you planning to say about my snatch?"

He gurgled from behind my hand and I could feel him smiling against my palm.

"If I remove my hand, will you tell me what you were going to say?"

He nodded his head up and down, but I didn't let go right away. He was lying back, propped up on his forearms so that his head didn't submerge, and I was straddling his waist.

"In this position, I could easily drown you," I threatened.

He nodded his head a little more vigorously and the dark wet strands of his hair flopped about, shaking drops of water onto my face. I closed my eyes for a split second and Joe took the opportunity to try to drown us both. He flattened out his arms and we went crashing into the water. There was some tossing and turning, and then we were all laughter and giggles.

When the silliness subsided, we got out of the water and laid out on one of the gray rocks that was situated at the water's edge. This was normal. Joe and I, eyes closed, side by side on the rocks, baking in the sun.

I reached for his hand, wove my fingers through his, and said, "I'm gonna miss you."

"You'll be fine." He turned his head to face me and I did the same. "You're not even that worried about it."

I felt my face fall. How did he know?

"Come on, Lua, I've been your best friend since before you could talk." His voice was soft and sweet. He wasn't angry. "I know what your fear looks like—this isn't fear."

I felt my face puckering because I was going to cry. And then I was crying, not like sobbing, but all drippy. I sniffled, sat up, wrapped my arms around my shins, and rested my head on my knees. Joe rose next to me and put his hand on my back.

"I'm sorry," I whispered.

"Don't be. You're allowed secrets, Lua. We're all allowed secrets."

"It's not really a secret."

He was looking out at the lake. He found a pebble with his left hand and threw it—starting a ripple of ridges in the water. "Tell me if you want to... or don't. It's up to you." He threw another pebble.

I was absolutely going to tell him but didn't speak right away. I was trying to find my words, but he was impatient.

"Oh my God, are you not going to tell me?" he said, utter shock in his voice.

I know he tried but he couldn't help himself and it totally lifted my guilt.

"No worries. I'm gonna tell you," I laughed.

And I did. I told him all about Bonnaroo and literal dick-head guy. I told him how embarrassed I was that I was still thinking about it—still daydreaming that I might see him again.

Joe was pretty positive about the whole thing, offering, "Listen, if nothing else, you're hot for someone who is not Lucas." Lucas was my ex. He also grew up on the thrive. When I was little, I thought I would marry him someday.

Lucas and Lua. I used to make Joe officiate at our fake weddings. Lucas and I started dating when we were sixteen. We were together for almost two years but as soon as he mainstreamed and went to the community college, he dropped me like a hot potato. I was pretty devastated, and since then, I haven't dated much. Even though our break-up was two years ago, Joe still hasn't said a word to Lucas, like not one, and they were close. It's messed up.

"I'm over Lucas. I keep trying to tell you that."

"I hear ya. But he's an ass, and honestly, I haven't heard you get excited about anyone since then, except Mr. Nameless Dickhead from Bonnaroo. So, I love him already."

"It's Literal Dickhead, Joe. Get it right." He smiled at me but didn't laugh. It's tough to get Joe to laugh. I was trying to accept Joe's positive viewpoint but I couldn't quite seem to get there. "I guess you're right, but I mean, come on, I don't even know his name."

"Perhaps you do," he teased. "Perhaps his name really is Literal Dickhead."

I sucker-punched him in the upper arm. "Ouch." He stood. "What are you hitting me for, I'm not the one who left you all worked up and unrequited."

"Jerk." I stood too, brushing my hands across my bottom and legs so that the little grains of pebble that had adhered to my skin fell away, leaving little pink impressions in their wake.

"Foodgasm, now?" Joe queried as he pulled me into a hug. I nodded against his chest.

An hour and a half later, I was once again waiting around for Joe. We had eaten everything Joe packed. Mozzarella, tomatoes, and basil with olive oil and crusty bread, home-cured meats, olives, nuts, dried apricots, a generous slice of leftover veggie lasagna, and two huge brownies. Exhausted and stuffed, we decided to head back to my house to nap but Joe didn't quite make it. As soon as we reached the edge of the hill that leads down towards the thrive's farming fields, Joe dramatically collapsed in the tall grass, complaining that he wasn't going to make it. To be honest, he did look like he was in actual physical pain. He was lying on his back, knees pulled into his chest, groaning. Drama queen.

"Why did you let me stuff myself, Lua? Why?"

"Please, you are uncontrollable. Don't blame me." I plopped down next to him and watched the grass blow in the wind. After a few more groans, he rolled onto his side, facing me and started to twist a strand of my hair around his finger; it was something he'd done since we were kids and I found it endearing.

Without warning, he bounced back to our old conversation, "Maybe, we can look on the Bonnaroo website at the photos from the festival and find his name in a caption." It was a thought. It was more pro-active than I had been. I'd pretty much been on a media diet since Bonnaroo—wanting to soak up the thrive before I left for Hamilton.

"Maybe," I replied.

He popped up so fast, he startled me. All goofy and gangly, his feet bouncing, he grabbed my hand and took off running, leaving the picnic basket behind us.

I was heavy behind him, not quite prepared for our movement, and then suddenly, he stopped, and I kinda tripped forward, still caught in his inertia.

"What the hell, Joe?" I said, backing away from him. He didn't respond. Instead, he quizzically stared ahead in the direction of my house. I turned to see what he was looking at and there was a van parked in my driveway, and not like a regular van; it was a news van, complete with a station logo and a satellite dish.

Joe started to speak, "I wonder..." but as soon as he started speaking, he stopped because he noticed another van crunching its way down the gravel road that wound through the thrive. Their presence made me uncomfortable.

"What do you think—"

He answered before I finished my sentence, "Don't know."

We were both kind of flabbergasted. We weren't scared exactly, but news vans on the thrive didn't make sense. News vans at my house didn't make sense. It might be nothing bad, but it was something, and it pulled us away from our afternoon at the lake. Unable to deny our curiosity any longer, we started walking towards the house, but we moved slowly, tentatively, savoring the walk because it felt like change was at its end. I couldn't help myself. I just wanted to hold on to all the feelings that came before the news vans for a little while longer.

"Joe?"

"Yep."

"What were you going to say about my snatch?"

Made in United States
Orlando, FL
16 March 2023

31099806R00104